The Beckoning

~ Entangled ~
Breanna & Ethan
© 2016 Jill Sanders

Follow Jill online at:
Jill@JillSanders.com
Web: http://JillSanders.com
Twitter: @JillMSanders
Facebook: JillSandersBooks
Sign up for Jill's Newsletter @ JillSanders.com

Jill Sanders

Summary

Breanna is a reasonable woman. She doesn't believe in things like teleportation or time travel. But after months of suddenly finding herself in faraway places and living through events that haven't taken place yet, she's beginning to think there might actually be something beyond the normal.

Ethan never believed he'd be living in his brother's house, let alone with the woman that's haunted his dreams and every waking moment for the past few months.

Jill Sanders

The Beckoning

by
Jill Sanders

Prologue

Breanna Garrett stood on a massive front porch with no clue how she got there. Glancing around, she guessed that she was back in a place she'd sworn to never return. Staring back at her was the dark-haired woman who had haunted her dreams for the past few months. She felt like she was in a strange universe.

For the past few weeks, her entire world had been turned upside down. Everything she'd come to know and trust had been pulled out from under her feet.

First, she'd caught her boyfriend cheating, then the bastard had actually cost her her job. But that wasn't the worst of it. The very fabric of her normal world had just turned upside down and inside out. She'd always had the strange flashes, the moments when she seemed to be dreaming about events that would happen in the future. But now she'd started ending up places with no clue of how she'd gotten there or why.

But now, those green eyes looking back at her from across the porch had her believing in something more. If the dark-haired, green-eyed woman was real, what about the tall, brown-eyed, sexy man who'd also haunted her dreams?

Suddenly, her heart rate spiked, remembering what those dreams had held. Wondering if those, too, would come true just like this one had.

Chapter One

Several Days Earlier....

Brea stood on the floor of the television studio and looked around. Two years ago, when she'd walked into the studio for the first time, she'd been so nervous as her new boss, Willard, had explained all the equipment.

So much had changed over the years. Gone was the shy, meek, and uncertain girl. Brea was now a woman who knew how to get what she wanted, and went after it. But it had taken a lot of time and work.

At one point, she'd been a poster child for nerdy, awkward kids. Now her braces were gone and she had perfect blemish-free skin. She'd spent countless hours watching YouTube videos on how to apply makeup and practicing new techniques. She'd even learned how to do fun and exciting things with her hair. She'd turned into a beauty queen, but she still remembered the pain and hurt she'd gone through all those years until she'd finally matured.

Two years ago, she'd nailed the interview at WSB, even though she was fresh out of college with her associate degree in art.

For the past two years, she'd fought and worked harder than she'd ever done and tomorrow she started her new job as head anchor for WSB. Just thinking about it had shivers rushing down her spine.

She loved her current job as investigative journalist, but she'd always dreamed of being head anchor. And when Debra, the current head anchor, had taken maternity leave, she'd begged Willard until he'd given her the position.

She grabbed her bag and headed out into the rainy night, making her way slowly through the traffic to her new apartment, ten miles away from the studio.

She parked in her designated spot and grabbed her bag, but just as she was ready to get out, a bright flash of light hit her, causing her to double over in pain.

The next thing she knew she was standing in a brightly lit grocery store. From the looks of it, it was the middle of the day.

She'd never been in this store before. Had she blacked out? Was she dreaming?

A woman bumped into her, almost causing her to fall into a bin of tomatoes.

"Sorry," the woman murmured.

The woman had long straight dark hair. Her face was uniquely beautiful and her green eyes were mesmerizing.

The woman reached out to steady Brea, who was a little wobbly from the surprise of being in the grocery store.

She was shocked to see the woman's green eyes go completely white, as if someone had drained all the color from her irises. The woman's coloring disappeared until she was as white as a sheet.

"Hidden Creek holds your fate," she said, just before she slipped to the ground in a pile at Brea's feet.

Her words sent a shiver down Brea's spine, and she woke to find herself once again sitting in her parked car, outside her apartment building, as the rain fell on her windshield.

All her life she'd struggled with these flashes, but in the past few months, she'd had them more often. Shaking it off, she ran up the stairs and bumped solidly into Drew.

"What are you doing here?" She narrowed her eyes at her ex-boyfriend. She'd met him on assignment last year when he was the head of WBNR, WSB's rival station. One thing had led to another and they had started dating without Brea even knowing how she'd fallen for the overly protective, self-centered man.

"What?" He sighed and leaned against her door,

smiling over at her. "Can't a guy visit his ex?"

"No. Not when that guy is the same creep who cheated with three…"—she narrowed her eyes and counted the women she'd heard associated with him— "make that four other women."

He shrugged. "So, I'm not a one-woman kind of guy. Invite me in and I'll remind you why you went out with me in the first place."

Brea's blood began to boil. "Maybe some women find that charming, but not me." She sidestepped him and was trying to get her door open when his hand gripped her wrist.

"I heard you got the head anchor job at WSB."

She stilled. "So?" She glared over at him.

"So, you might want to think about playing nice with me." His smile grew slowly.

"Why?" Her eyes narrowed. "What does WBNR have to do with my new job?"

He shrugged, but she could tell he was hiding something. "I just think it would be much better for you if we were on…"—he leaned in and sniffed her hair— "better terms." His hand went to her waist and pulled her close. She felt his arousal against her hip and shivered with disgust.

Jerking her arm away and taking a step back, she finished opening her door. She walked inside and blocked him from entering.

"No, I think I like exactly where we left things.

You running away with your tail tucked firmly between your legs." She glared down at his pants, and smiled. "And me with my dignity." She slammed the door in his face and leaned against it.

The last time she'd seen him, he'd been running from their apartment in nothing but boxer shorts, jeans and shoes in hand, as she waved her favorite five iron in the air.

She'd allowed his—what did you call the woman your boyfriend was cheating on you with? Mistress? —to get dressed quickly and leave with some dignity. After all, it wasn't the woman's fault that Drew Debris was the sleazy, no-good, cheating scum that he was.

Although the other woman was Kelly Reynolds, a woman who worked at WSB and knew that she and Drew had been seeing one another for months. That he'd moved in with her less than two weeks prior to the incident.

All in all, she was far better off without Drew in her life. The relationship had started to become somewhat of a burden, and she'd been thinking of asking him for her keys back. She was pretty sure he'd used her place for his tryst with Kelly so that he'd get caught and have an out from their messed-up relationship.

Dumping her bag, she kicked off her heels and went into the kitchen for a glass of wine. She heated up a slice of pizza from last night's dinner in the oven while she sipped her wine.

Hidden Creek. She felt a shiver run down her body. Was there even such a place? She flipped open her laptop and did a quick search. There was a small town an hour away called Hidden Creek.

Eating her heated pizza, she took the next half hour to glance through images on the web. There were recent news articles from a local paper.

She felt the blood drain from her face when she saw that morning's article about a woman with "gifted powers" who had solved a murder. The image was a little blurry, but there was no doubt that it was the raven-haired, green-eyed woman she'd just seen fall at her feet.

The investigative journalist in her wanted to drive down and dig deeper, but she had to settle for what she could find online instead.

She read the article several times. It seemed that the woman, Christina Warren, had stumbled upon an old high school friend shortly after her friend's lover had killed her husband. She claimed that she'd known the incident had happened, even though she'd been across town, and had insights as to the wife's involvement.

The wife's lover had confessed after several hours of questioning, but the woman herself was not talking and had lawyered up pretty quickly.

Brea spent the next hour researching everything she could about the psychic, which wasn't much.

It appeared that she had recently moved back to Hidden Creek after both of her parents had perished tragically in a car accident. There were a few grainy photos of her as a young blonde woman, no doubt from a school yearbook or a newspaper clipping.

She read every piece of information she could on the woman, but by the time she crawled into bed that night, she was no closer to answers than before.

Had she just dreamed of being in Hidden Creek? She had always had those "dream" moments. They were almost like memories, except most of the time the events hadn't happened yet. In the past few months, she had gotten more and more of them and about people she didn't know. What did it all mean?

That night, after falling into bed, she was plagued by dreams. The same ones she'd been having for a few months.

The sexy dark-haired man with chocolate eyes moved towards her slowly. His eyes focused only on her. Then he reached out and touched her, and she felt herself melt under his hands.

Suddenly, he pushed her up against a wall, and his hands roamed over her until she moaned with pleasure.

Clothes disappeared quickly. Soon skin touched skin.

When she woke from the dream, she was hornier than even, leading her to believe that she just needed a man. Any man. Soon.

The next morning, she was exhausted, having got only a few hours of sleep.

When she walked into work, she was shocked to see Allison Verica sitting behind the news anchor desk, appearing to get ready to go live in less than an hour.

Karen, one of the makeup artists, grabbed Brea's arm and dragged her into a small conference room.

"Did they call you?" she whispered, glancing out the door as she shut it behind them.

"About?" Brea frowned.

"The take-over?"

Brea got a sinking feeling in her stomach. "What take-over?"

"WBNR's taken over WSB."

"What?" It almost came out as a scream, and Karen hushed her.

"Yes, first thing this morning. They stormed in here and let half the staff go."

Suddenly Drew's surprise visit last night made sense. "Is Drew…"

Karen nodded and let out a low growling sound. "He's the one that's been handing out pink slips."

"You?" she asked, but Karen shook her head.

"I guess I'm one of the lucky few."

Brea took a deep breath, closing her eyes. She knew what was coming. Maybe she should have invited him in last night… No, she would not take the low road to get what she wanted. Straightening her shoulders, she nudged her chin up and opened the door.

"Guess we'll see where I stand." She disappeared down the hallway to go find Drew and see if she still had a job.

***

Ethan Kincaid had found his calling at the tender age of seventeen when he'd joined the ROTC program. He'd discovered that he was born to be an elite warrior. His skills surpassed most in his class. So, naturally, he'd joined up after graduation while his brother, Michael, had gone a different direction.

During basic training, he'd been head of his squad. After, they'd sent him on secret mission after secret mission until, one day, they made him a squad leader.

His uncanny foresight into a mission had been a huge asset. Soon, he began to think that he'd learned that skill instead of it being a freak of nature. It had always been part of his life and was something he'd hid from even his brother.

He'd first noticed his "hidden skill" when he and Mike had been picked on by Travis Pence, a bully in grade school.

Travis and his buddies had been planning to jump them on their way home. At least that's what his gut had told him. So, he'd pulled his brother to the soccer field that day after school for an impromptu game, which had taken them a completely different route home.

All that week, he'd dragged his brother different places until finally Mike stopped him.

"What's going on?"

He'd told him that he'd overheard Travis talking about beating them up, but that was a lie.

He'd never heard anyone talking about it. Instead, he'd just... known.

He wasn't even one hundred percent sure of it himself until Mike confronted Travis, who confessed everything.

At first, he'd thought of it kind of as a super-power, but then it had grown annoying. Knowing how to avoid tests or whether a girl would say yes or no if he asked her out had been helpful, but other times, it had caused trouble. People didn't like it when you knew too much.

He'd been the one to warn his brother that his best friend and partner on the force, Cameron, was going to betray him and try to kill him. All for a quarter of million dollars in drug money.

He'd called his brother less than an hour before Mike shot and killed Cameron in a dark alley. Mike had already guessed Cameron's involvement in the missing money, but he hadn't known that Cameron was on to him.

When Ethan called, Mike had gone on high alert. He'd let his partner lead him into the trap, but Cameron had ended up paying the ultimate price.

Mike had moved out of Atlanta to a small town about an hour away, and then things had started to get really strange.

Along with his uncanny second sight, he'd started having dreams of a silver-eyed woman, who called to him.

No matter what he did, he couldn't shake those dreams. Then they started happening to him while he was awake. It was making it hard to concentrate and he was losing track of time.

He'd thought about holding back and not going on missions, but then... duty called. Besides, he was pretty sure he just needed a break. He scheduled one after his next mission.

Jill Sanders

Chapter Two

The morning after the station's take-over, Brea found herself almost a hundred miles away in Hidden Creek, Georgia. She felt like she was about to pass out. She still had a job, thanks to some very quick thinking and all the research she'd done last night about Christina Warren and Hidden Creek.

Drew had been about to give her walking papers when she'd pitched an idea even he couldn't turn down.

An insider scoop on the mental stability of a psychic, or a woman claiming to be one.

The news of Christina Warren had even hit the papers in Atlanta. As of today, everyone in the state of Georgia was talking about Hidden Creek.

Naturally, she'd told Drew she'd front the cost of her trip as long as he promised that if he liked the story, he'd keep her on as a freelance investigative journalist.

He'd narrowed his beady eyes at her and,

thanks to some choice words from Willard, had agreed.

Whether she liked it or not, Drew was now her new boss. Could life get any worse?

She'd checked into a hole-in-the-wall hotel on the outskirts of town off Highway 23. It appeared to be the very same hotel in which Laura Schmitt, and her lover, Ray McGaven, had murdered Laura's husband, Daniel, in cold blood for three million in insurance money.

The yellow police tape was still hanging up a few doors down on room number 18.

When she walked into her room, she shivered and thought about sleeping in her car instead. But common sense took over and she tossed her small bag on the tattered comforter. The bed didn't even bounce, and she knew she was due for a long and sleepless night.

There was a small kitchen area with a fridge, sink, and stove, and she thought about stocking the fridge with some items.

Suddenly, she was standing in a brightly lit room. She had to blink several times for her eyes to adjust. Her entire body tingled, like she'd just stepped into a hot shower after being frozen.

She was so disoriented, that when she turned slightly, she bumped solidly into someone.

"Sorry," a woman's voice said.

She turned towards her and held her breath as she looked into green eyes. She tried to take in every detail, but before she could blink, the woman fell before her.

She reached out and caught her just before the woman's head hit the side of a wood case holding a bunch of tomatoes. Someone screamed, and several people rushed towards her.

"What happened?" someone asked.

"I... she just passed out."

A very large blond man stepped forward. "Christina?" He slapped the woman gently on her cheeks, then shook his head. "Someone go grab Jessie." A young kid took off quickly.

She sat there, looking down at the woman. At Christina.

"Is she okay?" She looked up at the man.

"Sure, she does this all the time." He frowned at her. "You're new in town. Did you touch her?"

Something close to shock must have crossed her face, because the man just shook his head and chuckled. He shifted, then easily picked her up. "We'll take care of her." He winked at her and started walking away with the woman tucked in his massive arms. He stopped and glanced back at her. "If you're sticking around, swing by the liquor store. I work the evening shift." His smile widened. "I'll make sure to give you a visitor's discount."

She shivered once more as the man walked away. She moved to the window and saw a sandy-haired woman rush from Coffee Corner, a place a few doors down. She reached over and felt

Christina's forehead, then nodded towards a truck. Brea watched the pair slide the unconscious woman in the back of the car. The woman climbed in next to her, then the man jumped behind the wheel and they took off.

"That happens a lot with them," someone said from behind her. She almost jumped but caught herself in time.

"Will she be okay?" She turned to the older woman and smiled.

"She'll be fine. I'm Clara." She smiled and turned towards Brea. "I work at Café 23." She pointed across the street from the Coffee Corner. "You're new in town?"

She tried to calm herself down by taking a few deep breaths. "Yes, I'm a reporter." This was real. It was happening. Now.

"Oh?" Clara frowned. "I suppose you're in town to report on that mess that went on a few days back." She nodded, her eyes once more going to the place where the truck had disappeared down the road. "It's a shame," Clara said, handing her a basket. "Walk with me while you do your shopping." It wasn't a request, so Brea decided to fall in step with the woman.

"If you ask me, Laura only married Daniel Schmitt for one thing." She waited as the woman picked up a loaf of bread and tossed it in Brea's basket. "Money," she said under her breath. "Everyone knows that the Schmitts had loads of it.

That girl was one of the most popular kids ever to barely graduate Hidden Creek High." She shook her head and added a jar of peanut butter and a jar of jelly into Brea's basket. She stopped when Brea frowned down at it. "You're not allergic to peanuts, are you?"

"N-No, but I prefer creamy instead of crunchy."

Clara shook her head and then swapped out the bottles. Brea continued to follow her through the aisles as she told Brea everything she knew about almost everyone in town, all while filling her basket with food Brea never would have purchased herself. To be honest, she doubted her little kitchen would accommodate the meals she was accustomed to cooking.

Less than an hour later, she left the store loaded down with finger food and a bunch of microwave meals. She'd been lucky enough to find her credit card in her back pocket, where she'd put it after paying for gas on her trip to Hidden Creek. Her purse was still in her hotel room along with her car keys. She'd walked the mile back to the hotel and, after asking the clerk to let her back into her room, she ran over the events of the last hour. The woman, Clara, had given her the scoop on the whole town, including Christina Warren and her new boyfriend, Michael Kincaid. She was still unsure how she'd ended up in the store in the first place, but remembered the day she'd dreamed of being there. Of having the exact situation happening.

Only after unloading all her new groceries did she realize that things had been different than in her dream.

Nothing she'd ever "dreamed" about had changed before. She sat down at her laptop and pulled out her notes.

She'd started writing a journal of her dreams shortly after her fifteenth birthday. Her father had taken her to a counselor who had suggested she jot them down and compare them to real life. Then she would see that she wasn't actually seeing the future, but just daydreaming.

If anything, her journals had done the opposite. One hundred percent of the time, everything she'd ever dreamed had come true. All but this one time. This one small detail.

Christina hadn't said, "Hidden Creek holds your fate" today before she'd passed out, nor had her eyes turned milky white.

Just remembering that part made Brea shiver. She took her time making her daily entry and then moved onto more research.

She was feeling a little tired and thought about flipping on the television and clocking out for a while, but suddenly, she felt her skin prickle.

She quickly grabbed her purse from the table. No way was she going to be left somewhere without what she needed.

Suddenly, she blinked against bright lights and

looked up to see the words "Police Station" hanging over the door she was standing in front of.

She made a mental note that her skin tingled, like before, and she also took note of her entire body and what she'd been thinking of beforehand. Then she glanced down and smiled when she saw her purse was still in her hands. Score one for her.

"Well," she said to herself, "looks like I'm visiting the police tonight." She wondered if she would magically appear here again if she walked back to her hotel.

She was too tired to make the trek back to the hotel right now, so she decided not to fight it and opened the door to the station and stepped in.

When she walked in, there was a small party going on. Blue streamers and balloons hung from the ceiling.

The small waiting room was full of people celebrating.

Walking up to the counter, she smiled at the woman sitting behind it, eating a piece of cake.

"Hi, I'd like to speak with the officer in charge of the Schmitt case." She held out her photo ID for the woman. So, she'd forgotten to turn in her WSB journalist ID. It wasn't as if Drew had asked for it.

"That would be Jacob," the woman said through a mouthful of cake. "Sorry, we're celebrating Terry and Kelly's baby." She leaned forward and smiled. "They say that girl, the psychic, told them it's a boy." She leaned back and shook her head. "Any reason to eat free cake." She shoved another forkful into her mouth and pointed with the empty utensil. "Jacob's there." She pointed to a tall good-looking man with dark brown hair. He was standing around, frowning at the people celebrating.

"Thank you." She walked away from the woman and made her way across the room towards the officer.

"Are you Jacob?" She leaned closer and read his badge. "St. Clair?"

When she said his last name, he frowned even more. "I'm Jacob. What can I..." He dropped off when she showed him her ID. Then he sighed and ran his hands through his hair. The move was sexy as hell, stirring something deep in Brea's mind and causing her body to react almost instantly.

Before she knew what was happening, he took her arm and pulled her into a side room, then shut the door, closing out all the sounds of the party.

"I'd hoped to keep this quiet, but I guess that was too much to ask for."

"Mr.—"

"Just call me Jacob." He frowned as he leaned against a desk. "And you were..." His eyes narrowed.

"Breanna," she supplied. "I'm with WSB, a WBNR affiliate out of Atlanta."

He nodded, crossing his arms over his chest. Her mouth went dry and her mind turned to jelly. What the hell was wrong with her?

Clearing her mind and her throat, she pulled out her phone from her purse, then held it up. "Is it okay if I record this?"

He took a deep breath and nodded.

An hour later, she let herself back into her hotel room. Tossing down her keys, she pulled out a frozen meal and heated it, then yanked off her shoes and wiggled her toes. The walk back to the hotel had been a long one. The shoes she was wearing were for looks, not a three-mile hike.

Sitting down, she flipped open her laptop and started typing. She only stopped to grab her food and a soda.

By the time she had everything down, the room was dark and she was fighting off sleep. Instead of crawling into bed, she picked up her phone, punched in Drew's number, and waited.

"I'm here. I'm sending you my first report," she said when he finally picked up.

"Jesus Christ, Brea. It's…" She could tell he was looking at the clock. "Two in the morning."

"Well, yeah, I got a late start. Besides, you did tell me that you wanted me to inform you of my every move." She smiled and wondered if she'd also woken up whoever was currently lying next to her ex.

"Yeah, fine. Call me tomorrow."

"Drew," she said, stopping him from hanging up. "I wouldn't have slept with you even if I'd known you were going to take over the station."

She could just imagine him smiling and felt her teeth grit.

"Sure," he said sarcastically. "Guess that's why I'm keeping you around. It gives me something to work for."

She hung up without batting an eye.

Deciding she would rather fall asleep in her clothes than crawl between the sheets and chance whatever was in there waiting for her, she rested on top of the comforter and closed her eyes.

As she drifted off to sleep, she thought about running into Christina at the grocery store. About the differences between her dream and reality. What did it mean? She thought about how twice today she'd... teleported. She shivered and tried not to think about it.

"Hidden Creek holds your fate," Christina had said in her dream.

She felt her entire body slowly relax as she let her mind settle.

Suddenly, she found herself in a dark field. The bright stars and moon shone above her, making everything glow, showing her the way as she walked. She didn't know what kept her moving forward, only that it was important.

She stopped at the opening of a large cave, feeling something beckoning her inward. Step after step, she moved as if in a trance.

When she entered, she realized it wasn't a

natural cave, but a tunnel. The entrance had been covered with thick brush, but when she entered, some light shone through, sending an eerie red haze to light her way.

She was just inside the mouth of the tunnel when a bright white light turned on at the end, blinding her and sending her falling to her knees.

Her hands and knees screamed out as she fell onto the rocky ground. Small, sharp pebbles buried themselves deep under the first layer of her skin.

She cried out as the bright light got closer to her. She shielded her eyes so it wouldn't blind her, but even then, the light seared into her mind.

She woke, screaming and breathless.

Jumping up, she turned on the light. Once the brightness washed over her, she saw that her hands were bleeding. Rushing into the bathroom, she glanced down at her clothes and frowned when she saw fresh mud and a huge rip in the knees of her jeans.

***

Ethan lay in his barracks after a full day of travel. In fewer than fifteen hours, they'd ship out from the base in Germany. Only he and his men knew where their next stop would be.

He ran over the plans in his mind. Everything should run smoothly. Then why did he have a nagging feeling in his gut that something had already turned against them? Maybe he should tell his commanding officer.

What? What would he say? Sir, I have this feeling. Shit!

31

He rolled over and shut his eyes, then took a couple deep breaths.

Instead of the stale smell of men, clean wool blankets, and floor cleaner, he was bombarded with the soft scent of a woman in a shower.

Opening his eyes, he blinked a few times as the water dripped from his face. There, standing less than a foot from him, was the most beautiful woman he'd ever seen. Her eyes were closed as the water washed over her face and long hair. She was facing slightly away from him, so he couldn't see much more than her perfect backside and the profile of her face. His eyes ran over her and he noticed she had a small tattoo on her right hip of three circles, all tangled with one another.

The shower was... hell, he knew this shower. It was at Mike's new place. What the hell was he doing in Hidden Creek? And who was this sexy woman standing naked in front of him.

Just then, she turned slightly towards him, her eyes slid open, and a slow smile formed on her lips.

"You're not supposed to get that wet," she said, glancing down at his arm.

He looked down and saw a white bandage covering his upper arm and shoulder. It jarred him awake from the dream.

Blinking a few times, he focused on Nick's face, one of the guys in his fireteam.

"Sorry, sir." He smiled. "Sounds like it was a good dream. But, it's time." He nodded, then turned and left.

Ethan sat up, rubbing his hands over his face. Glancing down at his shoulder, he sighed and wondered what the hell was wrong with him.

Jill Sanders

Chapter Three

Brea stood under the hot shower for as long as she could, her mind racing over what she'd seen. Had she really transported to that tunnel, like she had to the store and the police station? Or had it been a dream incident?

She glanced down at her feet. She'd woken with her shoes off. Wouldn't her feet be cut up from the sharp rocks? She sat on the edge of the tub and looked at the bottom of her feet. They were perfect. No cuts, no scrapes.

When she'd appeared in the grocery store, she'd been exactly as she had been moments before. And again, at the police station, she'd had her purse, which she'd grabbed right before arriving there.

She was seriously thinking about keeping her keys and a credit card on her at all times. It might not even hurt to sleep with her tennis shoes on.

She glanced down at herself now and cringed when she thought of appearing somewhere like she was now.

Flipping off the water, she grabbed a towel and dressed in record time.

Nothing was making sense. If only there was a clue as to why she was disappearing and reappearing places.

First, it had been to the grocery store to fulfill her dream. Then she had appeared at the police station, which she hadn't dreamed about at all. As she sat down to her computer, she thought about making a trip there to check in. After all, it was standard practice when doing research on a crime.

It was almost an hour before the sun would be up, and she spent that time digging deeper into the town of Hidden Creek.

Over the years, there had been plenty of strange things that had happened in town, but none of them were this odd. A group of teenagers had disappeared in the late eighties, but the official ruling was they had run away and joined a cult.

There were small, everyday crimes, but nothing out of the ordinary. She reread everything she could find on the Warren's car accident, but so far, she hadn't found anything other than the fact that it had been ruled an accident.

At sunup, she was even more tired than before falling into bed. Her phone rang at nine, and she groaned when she was Drew's number on the screen.

"What's this crap you sent me?" he said when she answered.

"Hello, Drew." She closed her eyes and rested her head on the desk.

"You call this investigative journalism?"

"Which part?" She sighed and flipped open the file she'd sent him.

"Everything. Have you interviewed this Christina Warren yet? What about the wife?" She heard his computer keys punching away. "Laura? How do we know they aren't in it together?"

"Well, as it clearly says in my—"

"I've read it three times. I'm telling you, there aren't any hard facts. Get some before you send me anything else." The line went dead and she wondered what she'd seen in the man in the first place.

Pulling out a blueberry yogurt, she decided to hit the pavement.

***

By the end of the day, she was exhausted. She'd had a sandwich at Café 23 and talked to the locals, but everything she learned was gossip at best.

There'd been no more teleportation incidents that day, but she didn't want to chance it anyway and kept on her shoes and clothes as she crawled onto the bed.

She was even too tired to jot down notes from the day. Her mind slipped into sleep, and she'd been out less than an hour when pain woke her.

She doubled over as a bright light seared into her mind. Then, as quickly as it came, it was gone.

When she opened her eyes. She was standing in a field, and someone was holding her hand. Something was calling her away from that

37

moment. When she looked over, the light hit her once more, causing her to double over in pain again. Then there was only darkness.

The only thing she'd been able to make out was a pair of sexy chocolate eyes.

She must have drifted off to sleep again, because this time, when she peeked one eye open, she saw the alarm clock in her hotel room.

Getting up, she felt like punching something. She was getting tired of things happening to her that she had no control over.

Once more, she was up before dawn with no hope of falling back asleep. She picked up the phone and called the one person who'd always steadied her.

"Hey, Daddy," she said, leaning back.

"Hey, pumpkin." Just hearing her father's voice settled her nerves. "How's it going?"

"Not so great. Did you hear about the take-over this week?" She figured she'd start with something simple.

"No, I've been stuck in meetings all week on some last minute changes of a bill. What's going on?"

For the next fifteen minutes, she filled her father in on her career, or lack thereof.

"So, where exactly are you?"

"Some podunk town called Hidden Creek."

The line was silent.

"Dad?"

"Yeah, I'm here, sweetie." Her father's voice sounded funny. So much so that her investigative side came out.

"Have you heard of it?"

"I lived there for a few years when I was in high school."

"You did?" She sat up. "Why didn't you ever tell me?"

"Well, I didn't tell you about the other twenty towns your grandparents dragged me to either," he joked.

Realizing he was right, she leaned back. Her grandfather had been a fortune hunter. He'd seen dollar signs every place except for where he was. He'd moved her father's family around so much, she wasn't even sure her father remembered all of the towns he'd lived in.

"So, what do you remember about this place?"

"Not a lot. Listen, honey, I've got to go," he broke in. "Stay safe."

He got off the phone quickly, leaving her wondering what her father hadn't wanted to tell her about the small town. She knew the man too well to fall for his act. Her father was hiding something.

Clicking her own keyboard, she typed in her father's name and Hidden Creek.

Several websites came up, wanting her to pay for searches, but she knew how to go around them. Finally, she found a picture of her father and mother. But when she looked closer, she froze.

Once more, she felt her skin tingle. She closed her eyes, wondering where she'd end up.

She'd been planning for this. Tucked in her pockets was everything she needed.

She was happily surprised this time, however, when she opened her eyes and noticed that she was standing outside of the local library.

Glancing down at her watch, she frowned when she noticed that it was five minutes after they had opened their doors. Where had the last two hours gone? Maybe she'd spent more time on her computer than she'd thought.

Regardless, it was just the place she wanted to be. She'd been thinking about stopping by the local newspaper office, as well, but the library was going to be her first stop.

Could she actually be getting a handle on controlling this?

Glancing around, she wondered if anyone had seen her magically appear, but the small town appeared to be completely quiet that morning.

When she walked into the library, she was greeted by an older woman. After telling the woman that she wanted to learn more about Hidden Creek, she was escorted into a large room in the basement.

Brea shivered slightly when she realized that the place resembled the library in the opening scene of Ghost Busters. The librarian showed her how to use the microfiche reader and pointed out where the films related to the town were.

The librarian told her that local papers published between ten and fifty years ago were all on microfiche and were labeled and organized in large wood file cabinets. Due to a lack of funds, most of the old newspapers hadn't been scanned into the computer system yet.

She researched the town for several hours. By the time she was done, her eyes stung, her head hurt, and she was pretty sure she was going to walk with a hunch for the next few days. She couldn't believe this was how people used to do research before the internet.

She spent the next few days in the basement of the library. Each morning, after getting dressed, she would feel her skin tingle, and she'd appear in the same spot in front of the library. She had actually tried to intentionally send herself there just that morning, but when she had closed her eyes and wished herself there, nothing had happened. Just when she'd finally given up, her skin had begun to tingle.

She still hadn't found anything that could explain what was happening to her.

Every night she was woken by new dreams. She'd seen the brown-eyed man several times before, but had always believed he was just her dream guy. You know, the man every woman fantasizes about. Usually he's a mix of several men together. A little Chris Hemsworth, some Bradley Cooper, a touch of Channing Tatum, and even some vintage Harrison Ford just for fun. She wondered if he was real, but doubted it, since every dream she'd had of him was very sexual in nature.

She'd never done some of the things she dreamed of. Her sex life so far had been limited. She'd only had two lovers and neither of them had ever done to her what she dreamed about brown-eyes doing.

She'd first started dreaming about him when she started dating Drew. Her dream guy was the complete opposite of Drew, so she'd decided that her brain was telling her not to get too involved. She should have listened.

But now, since being in Hidden Creek, dream guy had been showing up every night.

Between him and dreams about Christina being in trouble, she was lucky if she got four hours of sleep each night.

One night, after a long day of research, she'd thought she'd rolled out of bed and reached for the bedside light. She'd instantly been bombarded with images.

She saw a dark room lit by candles, and a woman's figure lying on a table, as if it was an altar. Then she saw a large red metal door, and a group of people standing around her, chanting.

The rest of the night, she'd stayed up, waiting for the sirens to drive by. When they did, she got dressed quickly and followed them.

From her car, she watched the paramedics take two people to the ER.

Her heart skipped a beat when she noticed the woman's black hair.

What the hell was wrong with her?

She banged her hands on the steering wheel. Flipping the car around, she decided it was time to leave Hidden Creek.

She went back to the hotel and was packing her stuff when she saw something out of the corner of her eye in the bathroom mirror.

Her mother stood a few feet behind her. Spinning around, she stared into silver eyes, much like her own. Taking a step back, she realized that it wasn't her mother.

"Aunt Misty?" She took a step forward, her eyes on the figure who appeared to be floating just in front of the door.

When her aunt's eyes moved to hers, sadness overtook her. Falling to her knees, she wept as the image of her aunt disappeared.

She packed her bags faster than she had ever moved and was out the door and in her car less than five minutes later.

About an hour later, she was back in her own apartment. When she shut the door behind her, she locked it and relaxed. Closing her eyes, she took a deep breath and then another to steady herself.

She hadn't seen a ghost. She had kept telling herself that the entire ride home. She'd said it so much in her mind that she'd actually started believing the lie.

When her skin started to tingle, she cried out, "No!" She forced her mind to stay focused on her apartment, but it was too late. When she opened her eyes, she found herself back in Hidden Creek.

***

Ethan shifted his pack on his shoulders as a bead of sweat rolled down his back. They were several clicks from their destination and that strange feeling washed over him again. He'd been fighting it all day.

It wasn't as if he could will it away. Especially

since now, his gut was tied in knots. Even his men knew something was wrong. There were only four of them, trudging through an area the US military had no right to be. Hell, if they were caught, he was pretty sure all knowledge of them would be wiped clean and denied.

"Sarge, should we—"

He held up his fist, signaling silence. No one moved. No one even breathed.

Once again, images of the silver-eyed beauty flashed in his mind. *Shit. Get it together.*

Now wasn't the time to daydream about some sexy-as-hell woman.

Dropping his arm, he took one step, then another. Suddenly, his feet flew out from under him. Thoughts of his brother crossed his mind just before bullets flew by his head. Desert dust, red canyon rocks, and dirt flew around him, and there were several loud booms.

Then, his entire body was tossed as a bullet ripped through his pack, tearing through his shoulder. Searing pain shot up his arm and shoulder, tossing him back to the ground. Glancing down, he saw bone sticking out as blood trickled down his side.

The world tilted slightly. He heard his men screaming and fighting back, but the only thing going through his mind was his brother and the silver-eyed woman.

He lay there for a moment, before everything settled. Glancing over, he realized that if he didn't move, his entire team was going to end up six feet under.

He rolled over and grabbed his weapon and started firing with his good hand. One of his men grabbed his leg and started pulling him to safety as he continued to fire where he assumed the enemy was hiding.

When he felt his vision start to gray, he bit the inside of his lip and held on for as long as he could. He was tossed over someone's shoulder and carried. Shifting up, he made sure he could see behind them as he held his weapon at the ready.

Only when he was tossed in the back of the truck they'd traveled there in did he allow his body to react to the violence it had been through.

Once more, his vision grayed as pressure was applied to his wound and his men screamed instructions over him.

"Hang on, Sarge," Nick said, frowning down at him. He didn't need to look down. He knew it was bad by the way Nick was looking at him.

"Shit," he said. "Someone better call my mother," he said, just before blacking out.

When he came around, he was in an evac. He knew that there were drugs flowing through his system because everything was fuzzy. But he had one question that had to be answered.

"My men?" He almost growled it out.

"All safe. You're the only one injured," the medic said, patting him gently on his good shoulder. "Relax, you've just earned yourself a one-way ticket back to the States."

Jill Sanders

Chapter Four

Brea stood just outside the door on the large front porch. She didn't know why she'd appeared there. One minute she'd been in her apartment, and now she was standing here looking at Christina.

Once more, the tingling sensation flowed through her, but this time, a warm shot of air flowed over her as well. The strange feeling caused her to take a step backwards as everything started to tilt.

Christina rushed forward and grabbed her arm, then jerked back as if she'd been burned.

"Sorry." She frowned at her. "Are you okay?"

"I…"

Christina stood back, tucking her hands behind her back. "Welcome. Please come in." She motioned her into the room. When Brea glanced around the room and saw Jacob, she relaxed slightly.

"I…" She took one step into the room. "I didn't mean to interrupt your party." She glanced down and realized she'd lucked out that time, since she still held her purse.

Christina chuckled. "Actually, you're just in time, seeing as you're the guest of honor tonight."

She turned back to the dark-haired woman. A feeling of dread washed over her. She'd seen this night. This moment. Several times before.

She knew that from here on out, everything was going to change. She'd tried to fight it by leaving town, but she'd ended up right back here anyway.

"Forgive me." Christina folded her hands in front of her, making it clear to Brea that she was not going to get a handshake. "I'm Christina, but please, call me Xtina." The name fit the woman standing in front of her much better than Christina. "This is Jessie." She motioned to the woman Brea had seen earlier that week rushing out to help the unconscious Xtina after she had passed out in the grocery store. "This is Jacob."

"We've met," he said, moving away from the fireplace a step and nodding in her direction. There was still a slight frown on his lips, but his eyes looked like he was waiting for the punch line of a joke.

Brea nodded in his direction, then her eyes fell on the man sitting on the sofa in the dark corner. Her breath caught in her throat. "I saw you get hurt," she said, breaking into the woman's introductions, "but it was your shoulder…" Suddenly she realized what she'd just owned up to and clamped her mouth shut.

"It's okay," Christina said. "This is Mike. It was his twin brother, Ethan, that was hurt. He's okay and is on his way back to the States." Christina sighed and walked over to lay a hand on the injured man. There was a dog lying next to him, and one of his legs was propped up, covered in a large white bandage.

It was strange looking into the eyes she'd dreamed about, but knowing it wasn't him. She couldn't tear her eyes from his as Xtina invited her to sit. Taking the seat across from him, she shifted her attention back to Xtina.

"I…" Where did she start?

"Who are you?" Everyone turned to look at Jessie, who just shrugged her shoulders. "You may know her"—the woman looked at Jacob and her eyes narrowed— "but no one else in the room does."

"Sorry." She shifted slightly. "I'm Breanna Garrett."

Jessie's eyes narrowed. "And?"

She shifted again. "I'm from Atlanta. I work for WSB." She thought about the text message she'd sent to Drew about coming home and cringed. He'd probably drive by her place and see her car parked in her spot. Which reminded her that she

49

was stuck in Hidden Creek without a car. She held in the groan of frustration.

"Why are you in Hidden Creek?" Mike spoke for the first time, causing her to jump a little at the familiarity of his voice. She'd heard him—no, his brother—speak so often in her dreams.

"I..." She wondered that herself, but then decided a little truth couldn't hurt. "I'm here because of her." She turned to Xtina.

"Me?" For the first time since Brea had walked in, Xtina looked a little shocked.

"Yes, because of this." She pulled out the newspaper article from her bag.

"You're here for a story," Jessie finally said, her eyes narrowing towards Jacob. "You knew about this?"

Jacob, for his part, only shrugged. Brea watched as the side of his lips curved up and suddenly, something in her mind clicked.

"You're brothers?" she said out loud, her eyes going between the two men.

"Yes," Mike said after a moment, tilting his head slightly. "You said you saw Ethan get hurt."

It was so strange seeing him sitting across from her. It was a little too dark to see clearly, but still, she could see small differences between him and her dream man.

"Yes." She felt her face heat.

"It's okay, we all witnessed it. Like you," Xtina said, walking around and sitting beside Mike. Mike took her hand in his and instantly Brea could see that their connection was deep.

"I saw him get hurt," she said again.

"Did you see anything else?" Mike asked.

She shifted again, not comfortable telling him about the rest of her dreams about his brother. Or the fact that she'd just... what? Teleported from an hour away. She felt some of the blood drain from her face. She'd gotten used to appearing at the library, but that had been less than two miles away. She'd always imagined that there was some sort of limit on her travel. What if she ended up across the world?

"I... I saw you." She turned her eyes to Xtina. "In the grocery store."

"The day I passed out?" Xtina frowned.

"Before that," she admitted.

"I don't understand," Xtina said.

She took a deep breath and explained how she had visions of things before they happened. When she was done, the room was quiet. She left out the part of teleporting and about her other dreams.

"Has this happened to you before?" Xtina asked.

Brea bit her bottom lip. "Actually, I've always had... visions."

51

"That come true?" Jacob asked, sounding interested.

Her eyes met his and she nodded. "But nothing like this… it was different."

"How?" Xtina asked.

"In my vision…" She glanced around the room and realized everyone was listening to her intently. No one looked at her like she was crazy. Actually, just the opposite. "Before you passed out, your eyes went white and you told me that Hidden Creek holds my fate."

Jessie jumped up from her seat. Her face had turned pale. "I… have to…" She rushed from the room.

After Jessie left through the front door, Jacob stood up quickly.

"I'll go check on her." He followed her out the front door.

The room was silent for a while.

"I'm sorry, would you like some tea?" Xtina stood.

"No, thank you." She glanced at the woman. "I know this may sound strange, but is there anyway someone could give me a ride back into town?"

Mike spoke up. "Didn't you drive here?"

Brea took a deep breath. "This may sound strange, but… The last thing I remember is walking into my apartment in Atlanta."

Again, the room was silent.

Less than an hour later, Brea found herself standing in the middle of the living room in Mike's house, just across the field from Xtina's massive house.

"Mike's in the process of remodeling, so if you'll excuse the dust," Xtina said, setting down a bag. "These are some clothes I had packed up. Honestly, some of them are from Jessie." She rolled her eyes. "My friend thinks I don't have enough clothes."

Brea smiled slightly. "I don't feel right staying…"

Xtina held up her hand, stopping her. "You may not know this, but I too have"—she blinked a few times and took a deep breath— "strange powers. I've had them my entire life. I used to think that it was a curse." She shifted, then motioned to the sofa.

Mike had stayed behind at Xtina's house, since he needed to stay off his leg for a few days, so it was just the two of them.

Brea sat on the sofa across from Xtina as she sat in a large leather chair.

"Here." She held out her hands. "I'll show you." She wiggled her fingers, telling Brea that she wanted to hold her hand.

Brea hesitated for a second, but then her curiosity took hold and she reached out.

When their fingers touched, Brea felt a weird sensation rush through her.

"You had a very lonely childhood. It was just you and your father, whom you love very much."

Brea's eyebrows shot up. But Xtina wasn't done.

"Your job is on the line." Xtina frowned. "From your ex, Drew." She sighed. "What an ass." She shook her head. "Sorry, anyway, you've been having visions." Xtina's eyebrows drew closer together, but Brea took her hands away.

"Sorry," she mumbled.

"No, I should be the one who is apologizing." Xtina leaned back. "I can read other people's minds by touching them," she said after a moment.

"Everyone?" She leaned a little closer, growing more curious.

"Except Mike." She smiled. "It's so nice not hearing…" She sighed. "Everything. When I'm with him."

"You've had this your entire life?" she asked. When Xtina nodded, she took a deep breath and decided she could let a few more of her defenses slip. "I've had… dreams, since I was a kid."

"Dreams?" Xtina leaned forward and tilted her head.

"Visions, really. Of things that are going to happen."

"Like what happened in the grocery store?"

She nodded. "Yes, one moment I'm somewhere"—she shook her head— "and then the next I'm somewhere else." She made a hand motion. "Then, zoom, I'm back to where I started."

"What happens next?"

"Usually, within a day or two, what I saw, comes true."

"Every time?"

"Yes." She frowned. "The only thing that has ever changed…" She felt a shiver run up her spine. "When your eyes went white and you said, 'Hidden Creek holds your fate.'"

"I've been thinking about that," Xtina said, getting up and walking in front of the fireplace. "When I saw you in the grocery store, and again when I first saw you on my porch, your eyes were different."

"My eyes?" Brea asked.

"Yes, they were very… silver. Almost as if they were glowing."

She blinked a few times, not sure what to say.

"Had you… Both times, had you just… appeared?"

Brea thought about it. "Yes. I normally get this sensation. Like pins all over my skin. But I didn't know about my eyes. Sometimes I shut them because they hurt."

"Interesting."

Brea sighed. "It sucks. Here I am, more than sixty miles away from my bed, with no clothes, no car, not even my own toothbrush."

"I'm sorry this is happening, but I'm positive you're where you're supposed to be."

She sighed and leaned back, closing her eyes for a moment. "Yes, me too. I tried to fight it, and look at how I ended up." She laughed. "Stuck here with no comforts of home."

"But, you were here just the other day, in the grocery store," Xtina said.

"Yes, I was here until this morning."

"Why did you leave?"

Another shiver ran through Brea. "I saw something. Actually, someone."

"Who?"

Brea didn't want to answer. Because as odd as it was talking about transporting over a hundred miles away and having visions of the future, not to mention being able to read someone's mind by just touching them, seeing the ghost of your dead aunt was just crossing that crazy line.

She shook her head and leaned back. "I guess I was just spooked and tired. I drove home and then"—she shrugged— "was here."

"What time did you get home?" Xtina asked.

"Why?" She leaned up.

"Just curious."

"Well, it was around six."

"In the morning?"

"Yes." She felt her heart skip as she looked out the window. Then she felt all the blood drain from her face when she noticed that it was dark out. Still.

"It's almost eight at night," Xtina said slowly. "So, where have you been for the past…"—she glanced down at her watch and calculated—"fourteen hours."

"I could be wrong. I was there, watching you get carted out of the ambulance, then I went back…"

"Wait." Xtina walked over and stood in front of her. "The ambulance?" When Brea nodded, Xtina knelt down in front of her. "Breanna, that was two days ago."

Chapter Five

*E*than sat in his brother's car and watched the scenery fly by. Stuck in the States for the next six months. What could be more boring?

He hadn't always been such a thrill seeker. But after his first mission with the Special Forces, something had changed in him. He started living for each mission. Downtime was filled with training or thrill-seeking adventures with some of his crew.

He glanced down at his arm and shoulder. For the next six months, he'd struggle just to be able to lift a beer to his mouth.

He held the worry about the visions he'd been having for the past few months in the back of his mind. Something was wrong with him, and he knew the best way to get to the root of the problem was to isolate himself and figure it out.

Which he could do in Hidden Creek, if his

brother and his new girlfriend could keep to themselves.

"So, tell me about this woman," he asked, shifting until he got a better look at Mike.

Even though they were identical twins, there were slight differences. For one, Mike was right-handed, and Ethan was left-handed. Which was a good thing, since it was his right arm that was nestled in the sling at the moment.

Their noses were a little different, as well as their smiles. But what was really different was the fact that Ethan had bulked on the muscles during his combat training, while his brother had "gone soft," as he liked to joke.

"Xtina?" Mike glanced over. "You'll like her. She's…" His eyes met Ethan's. "Different."

"As in, two heads? Or she has a large tattoo on her face?"

Mike chuckled. "No, neither. Just different. In a good way." He turned off the highway. "Mom and Dad like her."

"Oh, well, then she must be different than all the other women you've brought home."

Mike glared at him. "You'll see."

Ethan rolled his eyes. "So, tell me about the other one. The one that's staying at your place."

"Brea?" Mike slowed down as they drove through Hidden Creek.

Ethan had been there a few times since his brother had moved here last year. He liked the small town, but he didn't want to let his brother know that little tidbit.

"Yeah, the one that you want me to stay with."

"Geez, it's not like I'm asking you to sleep with the lady."

Ethan chuckled. "Sorry, it's just... I was hoping for some quiet time." He looked down at his arm. "She's not a hovering type, is she?"

Mike shrugged. "I wouldn't know. We've only known her for four days."

"Jesus." Ethan sat up, and Mike glared over at him. "Sorry, I've been hanging around the guys too long." He sighed. His parents had never allowed them to use strong language growing up, but after being around his buddies too long, words had a way of slipping out. "You just met the lady and you're letting her stay at your place?"

"Yeah." Mike smiled. "You'll see. You'll like her."

Ethan thought Mike gave him a strange look, but they arrived at Mike's house before he could ask about it.

"Man, you got a lot done since last time."

"You should see the inside," Mike said, parking the car. "I just have the guest room to finish." He sighed. "Been kind of slow after..." He nodded to his leg.

"Yeah, what are the odds that we'd both get shot within a week of each other?"

Mike sighed and reached for the cane he'd been using to get around. Ethan thought he could have had it worse; he could have to hobble around like his brother.

"Here," he said, rushing out of the truck and helping Mike get out.

"I don't need your help." Mike pushed him away. "You're the invalid here." He motioned to Ethan's arm.

"This?" He chuckled. "Flesh wound."

Mike laughed. "Right, and this is just a scratch."

"Are you two done making light of your injuries yet?" a female voice said from behind him.

Ethan turned to see a dark-haired beauty walking towards them. Her green eyes were fixed on Mike, but she glanced briefly over at him and smiled before walking into his brother's waiting arms.

"You must be Xtina." He held out his hand, and noticed that she briefly hesitated before reaching out to take his in a quick handshake.

"Now, if you two will come in, Brea has made dinner." She turned and started to grab the bag from the back of the truck.

Before she could, he reached in with his good arm and threw it over his shoulder.

"You shouldn't..."

He turned, his eyebrows going up.

"Never mind. I know that look and know better than to argue with it." She smiled.

He followed them into his brother's place and set his duffle bag inside the door. He let out a low whistle.

There was new flooring, paint, and even pictures hanging on the walls. The place looked like a home instead of a science experiment like it had the last time he'd been there.

Then he saw the woman standing in the

kitchen and he froze.

His heart stopped in his chest and he was pretty sure that for the first time in his life, he was going to faint.

"Ethan, this is Brea." Mike's voice shook him from his stupor.

When she moved towards him, his first instincts were to rush over and kiss the woman. Then he shook his head clear. He was just happy that she was actually a real person. All this time, he'd begun to believe that he was losing it.

"No, you're not crazy." Just hearing her voice made his heartbeat return to normal.

"Um…" He didn't know what to say.

When she laughed, the warm rich sound of it woke him from his coma. He shook his head clear and relaxed. "I'm Ethan." He moved closer, his brother and Xtina all but forgotten.

"Yes, I know," she said as she set down a glass and walked towards him. "I've seen you." She tapped the side of her head. "As I'm sure you've seen me."

He nodded, not really understanding what he was giving away. He was still so shocked to find his dream girl standing in front of him.

***

Brea had been staying in Mike's place for a few days. Xtina had been kind enough to drive her back to her apartment and help her collect some necessities—her clothes, her computer, and most important, her car.

They had wanted to do an experiment while

they were there.

They'd hung out at her apartment until late that night, hoping she'd vanish in front of a video camera, but nothing had happened.

"I wonder if it was just a fluke?" she'd asked before heading back to Hidden Creek.

"Could be, or it could be that somehow you already knew you'd come back here."

"But what about all the times I showed up at the library. I'd already settled into the fact that I was going to do the research there, so why did I end up popping in instead of driving each day?"

"Good question." Xtina smiled over at her. "Guess someday we'll know the answer."

So, she'd stayed at Mike's house and settled into a pattern. She was still writing and sending Drew more information for the article every day. He complained that she didn't have any information he wanted, threatening her each time that he didn't see any reason to keep her on.

She'd interviewed Xtina about everything that had happened to her, and Drew seemed very interested in sending the crew down so she could do a piece on her kidnapping. But he was looking for the angle of her being crazy, which Brea just wasn't getting from the woman.

If Xtina was crazy, then so was she. Because currently standing in front of her was her dream guy. Wow, talk about being nervous.

His hair was shorter than she'd remembered it being in her visions. He was still wearing his military fatigues and looking damn sexy in them. Even with his arm in a sling, he looked ready to take on anything. Except her. His dark eyes held questions.

"How about a beer?" she asked, then walked over and pulled out two bottles.

"Can't," he said, setting a bottle of pills on the counter between them.

"Water it is then." She set one bottle back and grabbed a water bottle for him, then poured Xtina a glass of wine. "Dinner first, then we can try and find some answers."

He was still standing across the bar, watching her closely.

By the time they all sat down at the table, everyone was a little more relaxed. Mike filled Ethan in on what they'd been through in the past few weeks. She found it a little odd that he hadn't yet mentioned Xtina's abilities, or her own, for that fact.

After the chicken Alfredo was devoured, they moved into the living room, where Mike built a fire in the fireplace. They talked briefly about his plans to finish remodeling the house, but then everyone grew silent.

"So," she said nervously, "you've been having dreams?"

Ethan's eyes moved to hers and held them for a moment. "For the past few months. I've... seen you."

"And?"

She felt her face heat when his eyes moved over to her brother. He cleared his throat and shifted in his seat. "That's it."

She knew he was lying and knew that Mike and Xtina also guessed.

"Ethan, would you let me try something?" Xtina leaned forward. "I have an ability to see into people's minds. Everyone except Mike." She smiled over at Mike. "I'm curious…"

He leaned forward. "For real?" His eyes went back and forth between Xtina and his brother.

Mike smiled and nodded. "Yeah, guess I'm a big mystery to her." He wrapped his arm around Xtina's shoulders.

"That's because there's nothing up there." Ethan smiled. "Been telling him that for years."

Xtina laughed, then held out her hand. "Would you allow me to try?"

Brea saw Ethan hesitate for a split second, then reach across the space and lay his hands in hers.

Instantly, Xtina's green eyes turned an almost emerald green and became unfocused. Less than a minute later, Xtina broke the connection.

"You love your brother very much." She smiled and leaned back against Mike. "And you love your job."

Ethan's eyes narrowed. "You didn't see any…" Concern flooded his eyes.

"No, I know better than to go poking around in military secrets." Xtina smiled. "I kept to your family memories." Xtina's eyes moved to Brea. "And, I saw a few flashes of what you've seen." Her smile fell away. "And what those images have cost you." Her eyes flew to his shoulder.

Ethan's eyes narrowed. "I should have—"

Xtina broke in. "It wasn't your fault."

Ethan stopped and took a breath. "So." His eyes moved to Mike. "Anything you want to tell me?"

Mike sighed and reached for Xtina's hand. "Did Mom and Dad talk to you?"

Instead of answering, Ethan leaned closer. "I would've liked to hear it from you first."

Mike's eyebrows shot up. "Why me? It's their secret they kept from us all these years."

Ethan tilted his head. "Maybe we're talking about two different things."

"What are you talking about?" Mike asked.

Ethan chuckled. "Oh no, now you have to spill first."

The brothers looked at one another, then quickly did three quick games of rock-paper-scissors. Ethan won.

"Shoot." He leaned back and smiled.

"We have a brother," Mike shot out. "Jacob is two years older than us and lives in Hidden Creek. He's a police officer and really wants to meet you, if you're up to it."

"Whoa." Ethan held up his hand. "Slow down." He stood up and walked to the fireplace, running his hands through his short hair. "A brother?"

Mike nodded as he swallowed hard. "The summer before they started their senior year of high school. Our grandparents forced them to put him up for adoption. They didn't even get to see him."

"And he lives here? You've met him?" Again, Mike answered with a nod. "Have the folks?"

"Yeah." Mike looked like he wished he could get up and pace, but he rubbed his injured leg instead. "Yeah, they've met him a few times."

"And you're just getting around to telling me?" He glared down at his brother. "Why didn't they tell me when they picked me up from the VA hospital? Or during the two days I spent with them?"

Mike sighed. "You'd have to ask them."

Both brothers looked at one another for a while.

"What were you talking about?" Mike finally asked.

"Hmm?" Ethan turned his eyes away from the fire. "Oh, about her." He nodded to Xtina. "That you're in love."

Mike laughed. "They told you that but not that you have a secret brother?"

"Yeah." Ethan turned back to the fireplace.

"Maybe we should go. It looks like Ethan could use some rest." Xtina stood and handed Mike his cane.

After they left, Brea turned back to Ethan, who was standing over the fire, staring into it deeply. Suddenly, he turned towards her.

"Have you met him?" he asked.

"Yes." She reached over and took her wine glass from the coffee table.

"And?"

She chuckled. "What? He's nice. Actually, I met him before I met Mike." His eyes stayed on her for a while, then he walked over and sat across from her.

"You said you've had dreams too." She nodded slightly, then slowly wet her lips. He watched the movement.

"In them, were we…" She didn't wait for him to finish the question, but nodded her head again. "Yeah." His eyes went back to the fire. "Talk about feeling the pressure."

She chuckled, then stood up. "Well, I don't know about you, but I'm tired." She set her wine glass in the sink. "I don't know if your brother mentioned it, but the guest room isn't quite done yet. And, since I've been here for a few days, I took over the master—"

"I'll be okay," he broke in.

"You haven't seen it yet."

He shrugged. "Then I'll take the sofa."

She smiled. "It would probably be more comfortable. Good night, Ethan."

"Night, Brea." Just hearing him say her name did something to her insides.

Jill Sanders

Chapter Six

$\mathcal{E}$than stayed awake most of the night. His mind kept playing over and over what his brother had told him. They had another brother. An older brother. He didn't know what hurt worse, the fact that his parents had kept this a secret from them or the fact that he'd spent two nights at their house and they had left it up to Mike to tell him.

Around one in the morning, he pulled out his cell phone and punched an angry message to his folks. He wrote it and deleted it several times before finally sending a simple, "Call me in the morning" text.

Shortly after that, he drifted off to sleep. He wasn't like most guys who almost got killed fighting to protect his country. He didn't have nightmares where he relived the moment when he almost died over and over. Instead, all of his dreams were filled with her. Breanna. Every single dream he'd had for the past few months had been about Breanna.

He got a few hours of sleep before the dreams took over. Suddenly, he was up again, tossing and turning as images of her consumed him.

"You okay?" Her voice came from a few feet away. Peeling his eyes open, he watched her walk towards him.

He rolled towards her and ended up on the ground, his shoulder screaming at him when he landed directly on it.

"Woah." She rushed forward and helped him sit up. "Easy."

He chuckled through the pain. "Forgot where I was for a moment." He sat with his back against the sofa. Her hands were still on his bare shoulders.

Her eyes were glued to the bandage.

"You're bleeding." He heard the concern in her voice.

"I'm okay." He finally got his breath back, but her fingers were still running over his skin.

His skin burned where she touched him. Ached was more like it. His entire body ached for her to run her hands all over him. Just like she'd been doing in his dreams.

"I'll go get some new bandages." She left the room, then quickly returned with a box of bandages.

"Come." She motioned to him to sit back on the sofa.

He slowly sat down next to her, his entire body aching with each move. Her eyes moved over him as her hands got busy removing his bandages.

He remained still, almost holding his breath as her fingers brushed his skin.

"You know, you should really be more careful." She frowned as she continued working. He could tell she was being gentle, but still, the fall was causing the pain to spike. "You look like you're in pain." Her hands stilled as she frowned up at him. "Didn't you get some pills?"

"Yeah." He nodded over to the bottle of pills on the kitchen table. "Can't stand pills." He knew it sounded like he was whining, but he didn't care. The pain was slowly growing.

She grabbed the bottle and read the label and then dumped two pills into her hand. She went to get a glass of water.

When she walked over to him, he frowned up at her. "Listen…"

"We can do this the easy way or the hard way." She cocked her hip out and he laughed.

"Really, what's the hard way? You hold me down"—images of her doing just that flashed in his mind and his smile grew— "and force me to swallow them?"

Her eyes narrowed. Reaching down, she ran a finger over his forehead. Her finger moved slowly down his face, until it rested over his lips. He felt his heart skip several beats as her eyes focused on his lips.

She shifted slightly, until she was standing

between his legs. His hands moved up, wrapped around her thighs, and pulled her a step closer as her finger brushed against his bottom lip several times.

She bent down towards him, her lips hovering inches from his as her finger dipped into his mouth and he got his first taste of her.

Her eyes moved up to his and she smiled, just as she dropped the pills into his mouth. She held the glass up to him and backed off. Her eyebrows rose as she challenged him to spit the pills out.

He swallowed the pills and laughed until his sides hurt.

***

Brea's breath was knocked from her when she saw Ethan's smile. It was the first time since she'd actually met him—physically, for real—that he looked relaxed.

Sitting back down, she went back to work wrapping his upper shoulder and arm in fresh bandages.

"Where'd you learn to do this?" He nodded to his shoulder.

"School," she answered, then stopped. "First aid. Didn't you take first aid in school?"

He shrugged. "Sure, and again in training."

She finished cleaning and wrapping his shoulder. The fact that his muscles bulged under her fingers told her there wasn't permanent damage. She wasn't a doctor but hoped that she was right at least on this small point.

"So, has my brother..." He paused. "Have Mike or Xtina talked to you yet about why we would be having these… visions?"

"Not yet." She finished taping the bandage in place and leaned back.

He touched the fresh bandage and moved his arm slightly

"This is just some sort of crazy. I mean, I can't believe crazy stuff like this actually exists. Dreams that come true. People who can read minds. Like for real read minds. Is there anything else crazy like this going on?" He sighed and leaned back, rubbing his shoulder.

Brea sat forward. She'd told Xtina and Mike what she was capable of doing, but telling her dream guy that she believed she could teleport was just nuts. But she didn't want to keep things from him. Especially not this.

"I sometimes end up in places, without any memory of how I got there."

"What?" He glanced over at her, a strange look on his face. "Like sleepwalking?"

She took a deep breath. "I'm not sure. I've missed some time too."

"Missed…?" Ethan frowned.

"Two whole days. One minute I was standing in my apartment, then the next I was on Xtina's front porch, two nights later."

"You don't remember anything?" he asked, sitting forward.

"Other than my skin tingling, no." She looked down. "I… They believe that I didn't sleepwalk, but… teleported." She held her breath as he watched her.

To his credit, he didn't look at her like she was crazy. Instead, he looked like he was trying to solve a problem.

"What else happens to you when you... end up in other places?"

He got up and grabbed a bottle of beer for Breanna and a bottle of water for himself. He sat back down and took a big swig of his water.

"I don't really remember. Just that my skin tingles, then I appear somewhere else."

"Where else have you appeared?"

She took a sip of her beer, the coolness soothing her throat. It was strange to be sitting here, in a place she didn't want to be, talking to her dream man about teleporting.

"Well, um, the grocery store, the library, and Xtina's front porch. That's it so far."

"Nowhere else?" he asked after a moment.

She thought quickly about her dream and the tunnel, but then shook off the memory. It had been just a dream. She was sure of it now.

"No, nowhere else."

"Well, how about we finish this conversation in the morning." He stretched his good arm over his head. "I just can't seem to wrap my mind around much right now." He set the bottle down and kicked his feet back onto the sofa.

She set her half-empty beer down and got up. "You must be exhausted." She glanced over at his shoulder again, pleased that the bandages looked clean. "Good night."

"Night." His eyes met hers.

For a moment, she felt her heart kick.

"You okay?" he asked after a moment.

"Yeah, sure." She faked a smile. "Night." She went back into her room, closed the door, and leaned against the door.

What was she doing? Talking about all this craziness with Ethan. Then again, she'd told Xtina and Mike everything and hadn't felt weird about it.

But she hadn't dreamed about them the way she'd dreamed about Ethan.

Just remembering some of the dreams she'd had about him caused her entire body to heat.

She glanced at her clock and sighed. Two more hours until dawn. She knew there was no way she was going to get any more sleep, so she flipped open her laptop and wrote down everything that had happened to her that day—her feelings towards Ethan, some of the dreams she'd had that night, and what she'd told him.

When she was done, she climbed into the shower. It still got to her, standing in the same shower that she'd dreamed of being with Ethan in.

Did that mean those dreams would come true too?

It was beginning to be too much, with all the visions in her head. It was hard to know what was real. What was now.

Since she'd returned to Hidden Creek, things had changed. She'd changed. She found her mind slipping between the two realms, visions versus reality. And now that Ethan was there, she was finding it even harder to be grounded.

She needed to talk with her father again. She

had even more questions than the last time she'd talked to him.

Her research had only added to her confusion. Hours and hours in the library and she had almost too many questions. But now, she itched to add the others into her research.

She'd researched Xtina and her family. Her parents and Brea's had been friends in school. From what she could tell, shortly into their junior year of high school, their friendship dissolved.

Maybe she should open up to the others and ask them to help her. Then they could all find out why this was happening to them.

But the way that Xtina and the others talked, it was like they had just accepted their fates. They had asked her why she thought this was happening, but so far, no one had talked to her about anything deeper.

When she walked into the living room, Ethan stood at the stove, cooking eggs.

"Morning." She leaned on the bar. "Did you get any sleep?"

He shook his head. "You?"

"No. I've been doing some thinking."

"And?" He piled a spoonful of eggs onto a plate and set it in front of her, along with some toast and a glass of juice.

"What do you know about your parents?" she said, scooping up some eggs.

He laughed. "Apparently, not a lot. Why?"

"Because I think that what's happening to us, all of us, now, is our parents' fault."

Chapter Seven

*E*than leaned on Xtina's front porch, watching Brea pace as they waited for Xtina and Mike to return home.

"Why don't you sit down?" he asked, earning himself a glare. "Funny, somehow I just knew that you had a temper."

Her eyes narrowed even further. "You know…"

Just then, a car turned down the long drive.

"Hey," Xtina said, jumping out of the hybrid car and helping his brother out of the passenger side.

It was still a shock to see Mike using a cane. It was one thing for him to be hurt, but seeing Mike suffer was a lot harder.

When Mike had been on the police force in Atlanta, he'd always worried about him. But it was

Atlanta, not Afghanistan, or some of the other places he'd visited himself.

"Sorry, we had to go into town to the doctor," Xtina said, helping Mike to the porch.

"Is everything okay?" Instant worry shot through him.

"Yeah, great. Fine," Mike added between clenched teeth.

"It was my fault." Ethan could see the worry in Xtina's eyes. "I should have tied him to the bedpost."

Mike laughed. "Then we still would have had a visit to the doctor this morning." His brother's eyes caught Xtina's and for the first time, he could tell that his brother was in love.

"First of all... Ew, gross. TMI. Second, are you okay?"

"Yeah," he said after Xtina helped him sit down on the swing. "Could use some iced tea." He glanced over at Xtina.

"I'll be right back." Xtina disappeared, and Ethan was happy when Brea followed her into the house.

"Okay, spill." Ethan sat across from Mike. "What happened?"

He glanced down at the new bandages on his brother's leg.

"You first." He nodded to his own fresh bandages. Ethan reached up and rubbed his shoulder.

"Fell off the sofa."

"Fell out of bed," Mike said, chuckling. "Looks like we both should have been tied down."

Ethan's eyes narrowed. "I was sleeping on that thing you call a sofa. I'll wager your bed was a lot bigger and"—his eyes moved to the doorway—"that you weren't alone."

"Yeah, so. Still…" Mike rubbed his hand through his hair, much like Ethan did when he was troubled. "Shit happens."

Ethan's eyebrows rose. "Spill."

Mike sighed. "So, remember my ghost?"

"Yeah, the one I couldn't see." Mike nodded. "What about her?"

"She made an appearance last night."

"And?"

"Something's changed."

"What do you mean?"

"She's… different."

"How?" Ethan still didn't know if he believed in his brother's visions, but with all the other crazy things going on, he was more open to the idea than he had been a year ago.

Mike shook his head. "Later," he said in a low voice as Xtina and Brea walked out followed by a dog, who ran up to him and demanded to be petted.

"This is Rose," Mike said, catching the dog's attention. The border collie walked over and plopped herself down at Mike's feet.

Xtina held a tray full of iced tea and a plate of crackers and cheese.

"Here." She sat down and handed Mike two pills, making him remember his own meds were on the countertop. He had no plans to take them. Mike swallowed his down, and Ethan realized that he must be in pain.

"What brings you two over here?" Xtina asked as she poured four glasses of tea.

"It was my idea." Brea sat forward. "I told you I'd been doing some research, but I didn't get a chance to tell you on what. Or more to the point, on whom."

"Okay." Mike shifted slightly. "Want to tell us?"

"Actually, I think we should wait for the others to get here." Brea shifted her eyes to Ethan.

"You called Jessie and Jacob?" Mike's eyes moved to his.

"Shit," Ethan said, running his hands through his hair and glaring towards Brea. "You could have given me some warning."

"So you could talk me out of it? No. This had to happen sooner or later." She stopped as another car came up the drive.

"Yeah, just wish it was later," he said under his breath.

He watched as the brother he'd never met got out of a patrol car and walked towards them.

The second his eyes landed on him, he knew he was family. He looked just like their dad. More pain surfaced as he watched the man move towards them.

Then Jacob's gaze landed on his and he could see the same emotions behind the familiar eyes. He stopped at the base of the steps, so Ethan set his glass down and stood up.

"Ethan." He held out his good hand.

"Jacob St. Clair." He climbed the three steps and took his hand in his. "I've heard a lot about you."

"Funny, I just found out about you last night." His eyes landed on Mike, who looked a little sad and tired now.

"I wanted to tell you the second I found out," Mike said. "But you were…" He shrugged.

"Yeah, right." Ethan sat back down.

"So, what's this all about?" he asked Brea.

"First, we're waiting for Jessie." She sat down and Jacob sat next to her. Xtina poured him a glass of tea.

"No hints?" Xtina asked.

"No," Brea said, shaking her head.

"Jessie's shift doesn't end for about an hour," Xtina added.

"She said she was going to leave early," Jacob supplied. Everyone looked over at him.

"I stopped there for breakfast." Ethan could tell there was something he was hiding.

"Okay, so while we're waiting, why don't you tell me about…all of this." Ethan waved his hands between the five of them.

**

Xtina and Mike filled Ethan in on everything they knew as they waited for Jessie. Brea had heard their stories before. How they had seen the same things and how being together had affected them.

She still found it all a little… too much to grasp.

83

"Wait." Jacob sat forward, interrupting Xtina's story.

"You're telling me she can teleport and time travel?" Jacob leaned forward.

Brea blinked a few times. What? What had they said?

Every eye was on her and she felt a little uncomfortable. She didn't know what to say and was thankfully saved when a car drove up.

"Hey," Jessie said, walking up the stairs. "Looks like the gang's all here." She sat down across from Jacob and took a glass of tea. "So, what's this all about?"

Once again, everyone glanced over at her. This time, she did know what to say. She flipped open her laptop and turned it around.

"That's the picture from the yearbook," Jessie said, leaning forward.

"Yearbook?" Xtina asked.

Jessie disappeared into the house and returned holding a book. "Here." She flipped open the book to the same picture Brea had on her laptop.

"As far as I can tell, they're our parents. All of them." She pointed to her father and mother. "My father, Byron Garrett, and my mother, Dawn. This is my aunt Misty."

"This, is your aunt?" Xtina said, reaching for Mike's hand.

"Yes."

The next photo included everyone except Misty, and every person in this photo looked sad, like something major had just happened.

"Okay, so now we have a name for our..."

Mike said.

Ethan tapped the picture. "This woman is your ghost?"

"Not a ghost," both Mike and Xtina said at the same time.

"So, if it's your aunt that we keep seeing," Mike said, "then why? What does this all mean?"

"It means that they are the reason all of this is happening to us." She showed them another photo. This time, the entire gang was there. They were all wearing dark clothes and holding flashlights, like they were about to go on a grand adventure. Their smiles were big and they all looked so young and happy.

Suddenly, several people were talking at the same time.

"Okay, okay," Xtina said, raising her voice over the others. "Can we take this down a notch? Let's start at the beginning. There has to be something here that will lead us to answers."

"Well, if this is going to be a long day, how about we order some pizza?" Jessie said, propping her feet onto the railing. "What?" she said after everyone looked at her. "I'm starving."

"I'll call in an order." Xtina stood.

"We get delivery?" Mike asked. "I've lived here for over a year, and now I find out I can have pizza delivered?"

Xtina laughed and leaned down to kiss him. "You just have to know the right people." She disappeared into the house.

Mike turned to Breanna. "Can you shoot

everything you have to me?"

She thought of her other research, but knew she could keep that from him. "Sure." She typed in the email address that he read off.

"I'd like a copy too," Jacob said.

"Sure." She glanced over at Ethan.

"I'm good." He chuckled. "Let my brothers collect the data. I'm more of an action man myself."

Her face heated. She'd imagined exactly what kind of actions he could do for the past few months.

"So," Xtina said, walking back out. "Where do we start?"

"With this." She pulled up another picture, this one attached to a newspaper article.

It said, "Local teen disappears" above a picture of her aunt Misty.

They read through the article and then put together a calendar where they filled in past events.

"Your father, what has he said about this?" Jacob asked.

"Nothing. That's the thing. I can't get him to open up to me." Her eyes moved around. "What about any of you?"

"I tried to talk to our folks." Mike's eyes moved to his brother. "But they are closed lip about it. Of course, this was before I saw this." He tapped the photo in the yearbook. "I have a lot of new questions."

"And you?" Brea turned to Jessie.

Xtina reached over and took her friend's hand,

the first time Brea had seen Xtina do so.

"Jessie's parents are…"—she took a breath—"out of reach."

Brea glanced down at the photo of the young couple. Jessie looked a lot like her mother.

"Rachelle and Larry aren't your typical parents," Jess supplied as she stood up, dropping her friend's hand. "I haven't spoken to either of them since I was thirteen."

"Thirteen?" Jacob broke in. "Then who have you been living with?"

"I live by myself," she added, her chin going up slightly. "I have since they left."

"Since you were thirteen?" Jacob asked.

"Yes, St. Clair, you got a problem with that?" She crossed her arms over her chest, ready to defend herself.

"Hell ya, I do. You were just a kid. You shouldn't have been left alone."

"Jacob," Xtina interrupted, "she's had people looking out for her." Xtina winked at Jess. "She'll never be alone."

Brea could see the anger behind Jacob's eyes and knew that it wasn't over between them.

"So, let's start at the beginning again." Xtina pulled out a marker and started writing events on the chart in chronological order.

Chapter Eight

Two hours later, full of pizza and beer, they sat around Xtina's living room, going over every scrap of information Brea had. Ethan sat back and watched the show as everyone mulled over the information.

"So, what do we know?" Jacob asked, pacing the floor as he sipped on his beer. The way he moved was so much like his father and Mike that Ethan felt an ache in his heart that he had not grown up knowing his older brother.

He'd learned a lot about everyone from just watching them.

Like the fact that Jessie and Jacob acted like they couldn't stand one another, but were secretly totally infatuated with one another. So much so that the air around them almost sizzled.

He wondered if that's how it was when he and Breanna were alone. That's how it felt to him. He didn't know if it had anything to do with the visions, but he couldn't stop his mind or body from reacting when he was near her.

He'd caught her glancing at him several times, and he'd felt his entire body respond every time their eyes locked.

He likened it to a calm before the storm. All day long, the clouds had been building and, soon, lightning was bound to hit.

"Well, that was a lot to take in," he said as they walked across the yard towards his brother's place.

She had her laptop bag in her hands, along with the chart that Xtina and Jess had created.

"Yeah, I can't believe that Jess has been on her own since she was thirteen," Brea said, shifting the bag in her arms.

He reached over and took it from her.

"You're not supposed to use that." She frowned as he shifted the heavy bag to his good arm.

It was like a wave hit him in the knees, knocking him to his ass. One minute he was standing in the dark field, with fireflies buzzing around him, then the next he was butt naked, standing in a shower, looking at her in front of him.

Water dripped down her skin, making it glisten, as she smiled up at him. "You're not supposed to get that wet."

"Shit," he said, taking a step back.

Her hand reached out, stopping him from falling on his ass.

"Ethan?" She shook his good shoulder a few

times. "You okay?" She was standing in front of him, fully clothed, frowning at him.

"Yeah." He blinked a few times. It was like so many other visions he'd had before. He should have been able to shake it off, but something was different.

His knees went weak, and Brea snagged her computer bag from him seconds before he would have dropped it.

Vaguely, he heard her yell for help, but his entire world was tilting. Everything narrowed and dimmed before it turned dark.

"You're not taking your pills," she growled out. Her eyes were narrowed as she looked down at him.

Strange, the grassy field was as soft as a bed.

He brushed his thumb across the worry line between her eyes. "Sorry," he said, his voice sounding hollow.

She took his hand and that was when he realized he wasn't laying in the dark field, but in a bed in a dimly lit room. His brother's room.

"How'd I get here?" He tried to sit up, but she put her hand on his good shoulder.

"Don't move." She turned and said, "He's fine. Just the water and pills."

Jessie handed Brea both items while Jacob stood in the corner, his arms crossed over his chest.

"Hey, bro," he said. Seeing the smile, he knew that Jacob had carried him into the house. He felt like a fainting teenage girl.

"You can go." He almost barked it out.

"No, they can't. At least not until your coloring comes back." Brea stepped between him and his older brother, blocking his view of the gloating man.

"Swallow these." She shook out two pills and handed them to him.

He laughed. "I don't need..." A low sound came from her throat. His eyes met hers and something close to fear jumped into his chest.

Without saying another word, he took the pills and swallowed them down.

"Pussy whipped." Jacob laughed from across the room. "Both of them." He shook his head as he walked from the room.

"Thank you," Brea said to Jess. "Both of you." She nodded towards the door.

"Sure, if you need anything else..."

"We're fine," Brea said.

When the front door shut, she turned on him.

"Why aren't you taking your pills?"

"Because I don't need them." He shifted, and when the pain hit him again, he cringed. Okay, so the searing pain had been stabbing him all day. He's only been able to nibble on a slice of pizza, but he'd drank a whole beer. Didn't that count for anything?

When the room spun, he decided he'd better not move again. "Shit." He thought he'd only thought it, but suddenly she was back at his side.

"Are you okay?" She sat on the edge of the bed, her hand going to his good shoulder.

"Yeah, sure. Fine." He closed his eyes and rested his head back. "Tell me that Jacob... My brother didn't carry me in here."

She chuckled, the rich sound like honey. "Sorry, he was the only one big enough to carry you."

"You could have dragged me. Better yet, let me lay there in the field."

"And let the mosquitos get you?" He opened one eye, then the other when the room didn't turn.

"Sure, why not."

"Because I'm human and have a heart. Your color is back," she said after a moment.

That was probably because she was leaning over him and he'd noticed how close her perfect breasts were to him.

Before he could stop himself, he brushed a strand of her blonde hair away from her face. "I've dreamed about us," he said softly. When she didn't pull away, he nudged her forward, until she was a breath from him. "About this."

He let her make the move, and when her lips touched his, his hands wrapped around her waist, holding her to him.

Her mouth brushed over his, and he ran his tongue across her sealed lips. Then their tongues touched and he couldn't stop the moan from escaping.

She tasted just like he knew she would. Just like honey. Sweet, and extremely potent. He had to have more. His hand went up her body until it settled in her hair, holding her to him as he explored her mouth.

She was leaning on him now, her body pushed

tightly up against his. He wanted to explore her even more, but the movement of his shoulder was limited.

"I knew it would be like this," she said against his lips. "My god." She ran her hands over his chest as her lips brushed against his.

"More," he begged, not caring if it was a sign of weakness. He shifted, hoping to have her body under his, but the pain struck and soon he was flat on his back, looking up at the ceiling of the bedroom, breathing harder than before.

"Ethan." Her voice was right next to his ear.

"Damn it," he growled.

"Easy, don't move." He felt her hand holding his good shoulder down.

His eyes met hers. "Later." He didn't know if it was a warning or a promise. "We're going to see this through."

She smiled and relaxed slightly. "I'm not going anywhere," she said before his eyes slid closed and he fell into a drug-induced sleep.

***

Brea watched Ethan's eyes slide closed and sighed. Just her luck. Just when she gets wound up tight and ready for a release, the man she wants passes out, again.

She couldn't believe how kissing him had affected her. Hell, her lips were still on fire. She'd never been kissed like that before. Ever. And Ethan wasn't at one hundred percent. She was in major trouble when he finally recovered.

What did she do now? Her entire body was vibrating and he was out. On her bed.

She thought about sleeping on the sofa and how uncomfortable it would be.

No, she was determined to sleep in the bed. After all, he'd most likely sleep the entire night through. She'd read the pill bottle and had known that he'd be out shortly after taking them. Which was probably why he'd been avoiding them so far.

She pulled off his shoes and his socks and thought for a brief moment about pulling off his jeans. That would be crossing a line she wasn't ready for just yet.

She unbuttoned a few buttons on his shirt, changed into her silk shorts and matching tank top, brushed her teeth, and removed her makeup.

She was exhausted. Not just tired, but totally drained. When she walked back into the bedroom, Ethan had rolled over to his side, leaving her side of the bed free.

Pulling out an extra blanket, she tossed it lightly over Ethan before crawling under the sheets herself.

It was strange, on any normal night, she would toss and turn for a while before drifting off to sleep. But, tonight, she just blacked out.

The dream started like it had several times before. She was walking in an open field, determined to go somewhere, to do something important. The tall grass softened her footsteps as she walked. The waxing moon hung low in the sky.

She glanced over when she heard someone behind her. Ethan was walking towards her. He looked at her like she was a miracle. Like she was everything he'd ever wanted in life. His arm was no longer in a sling and he looked amazing.

When he was only a few feet away from her, their eyes met.

"You have to let me go," she whispered. Suddenly, she felt her skin start to tingle. Somehow, she knew that this would be the last time she saw Ethan. She tried to fight fading in front of him, but nothing could hold back fate. Not even love.

"Hey," Ethan's voice broke into the dream. He was warm and real next to her and she felt her body being shaken lightly. "Brea?"

She woke from the dream slowly. Ethan's hands were on her shoulders, his body pushed up against hers as he held her close.

She was so happy to be out of the dream and drew him to her, putting everything she had into the kiss, everything she'd been feeling moments before she'd woken. Her legs wrapped around his hips, pulling him closer.

Her fingers moved over his bare skin. He must have pulled his shirt off sometime during the night. She realized that his jeans were gone too when she felt him against her.

"Ethan." A small bit of sanity returned to her.

"No, Brea, let's ride it out." He moved slightly, and her entire body reacted as he pushed up against her silk shorts. His hand roamed over her body, pushing her tank top up. She arched back when his fingers brushed her bare skin.

She moaned his name when his lips left hers and traveled slowly down her face and neck. He finally reached the peak and took it into his mouth. She screamed this time as his mouth sent shock waves through her entire system.

His free hand moved down her ribs, her stomach. A finger dipped into her belly button, before running across the line of her shorts. One tug and the silk was down over her hips. Her body arched for him, desire controlling her every move.

Her legs parted, exposing her to his view.

"Beautiful," he whispered next to her skin. "Just as I dreamed." His fingers brushed over her skin and her eyes closed with pleasure.

"Ethan." She didn't know if she was begging him to stop or continue. At this point, all she knew was that something needed to extinguish the flames.

"I know," he said as he ran hot kisses down her ribs, following the same path where his fingers had just burned.

When his mouth replaced his hands, she completely lost it. Her body and mind opened.

A shooting soft light almost blinded her as her entire body lifted and pulsed. She'd never felt anything like it before, and something told her at that moment, that she never would again.

Chapter Nine

He doubted he would ever see anything as beautiful as Brea as she came back to earth. Her entire body glowed. Her eyes fluttered open and he smiled when he noticed how silver gray they were.

He shifted so his good shoulder was up against her and wrapped his bad arm around her gently. He held her close, enjoying the feel of her heartbeat settling against his skin.

"Ethan," she said against his chest.

"Hmm?" he said unable to hide the satisfaction in his tone.

"What... aren't..." His chuckle stopped her. "Is that it?"

He reached up and brushed her hair away from her face. "For now, it'll have to do. Come back down here. It's cold and I want to feel you next to me."

She settled next to him and sighed.

"I owe you," she whispered next to his chest.

He wanted to argue because, after all, she had given him so much. No, she didn't owe him. He was pretty sure at this point that he could never repay her.

He drifted into a dreamless slumber that lasted until the sun streamed into the room. He rolled over and was instantly attacked with sharp pain. His breath was almost knocked from him and is shoulder felt like it was on fire.

"Damn it," he growled out and sat up.

"Are you okay?" Vaguely, he was aware of Brea's hand touching him.

"Yeah, fine," he said between clenched teeth.

"I'll got get your medicine."

Damn it. He'd had other plans. Plans that included running his hands over every inch of her, enjoying how soft and warm she was. But now, the pain was so overpowering, he couldn't bear to even pry open his eyes.

"Here." She took his hand and dropped a few pills into it. "I have water."

Without questioning, he swallowed the pills and then lay back when she shifted the pillows behind him.

"You need to rest. You need time to heal."

He knew it, but what he wanted and what he needed were two different things.

Finally, he opened his eyes and felt his breath leave him for a second time that morning.

She was standing less than a foot away from him, the sunlight streaming into the window behind her, setting her blonde hair on fire. She'd donned his shirt, leaving all the buttons open, revealing the sexiest strip of skin that he'd ever seen.

"Come here." He was surprised at the croak in his voice.

"You're hurt." She bit her bottom lip, and he felt himself grow harder.

"Not so much that I can't enjoy looking at you."

She smiled and took a step towards him. "You need rest." Her eyes roamed over him and landed on his chest.

"Brea." Her eyes met his. "I want you so bad. I've dreamed of this moment." He wrapped his good arm around her hips, causing the shirt to fall open a little more. "What I need is right here." He slowly opened the shirt wider. He laid his lips against her soft skin and felt her melt.

Her fingers went into his hair, gently holding him to her breasts.

She tasted so good. Her skin was so soft, he doubted he could ever get his fill of her.

He nudged the shirt until it fell onto the floor in a pool of white. His eyes moved over every inch of her perfect skin, her perfect body. She was heavenly.

Before he could touch her again, she took a step back and put a hand to his chest.

"No." She shook her head, the sunlight streaming in behind her. "This time it's my turn." She gently placed a hand on his good shoulder and pushed lightly until he leaned back against the headboard.

She moved closer and straddled his hips. He still wore his boxers, but just feeling her naked body next to him was driving him crazy. She slowly trailed her mouth over his jaw line, then down his neck and his chest.

She pushed his boxer's down his hips, running her mouth over the skin she was exposing.

He couldn't take his eyes from her as she nudged the boxers off him. Her smile was quick when she laid eyes on what she was doing to him.

"I want you so much." He reached for her, but she leaned back and shook her head.

"Not yet. I told you last night that I owed you." It came out as a purr. Then she bit her bottom lip as she ran one fingertip over his chest, down each rib on his good side, and around his navel. He closed his eyes and released a moan when she trailed a finger down his length.

"You're killing me," he groaned. She wrapped her hand around him, and he almost jumped out of his skin when her lips followed.

"My god!" he groaned, his hand going into her hair. "My god!" he repeated as she used her sweet mouth on him.

She was taking him to the edge too fast.

He silently prayed that his brother would have him covered and reached for the nightstand drawer, smiling when he felt a box of condoms.

She leaned over and took the wrapper from him. "Let me."

"I'm not totally helpless," he joked as she slid the condom on him. He hissed with pleasure. "But, I have to say, being hurt does have some benefits."

His smile fell away when she straddled his hips. His hand went to her hips, holding her, guiding her.

When she slid down onto him, he felt his entire system shake. He never imagined she would feel this good. No matter how many times he'd dreamed about her, it had never compared to the real thing.

***

Brea closed her eyes and leaned back. She had completely lost control. The way he'd looked at her earlier still caused her body to vibrate.

She'd never been looked at like that before. Like she was the most beautiful thing on earth. She wanted to keep going, caution be damned.

He felt too good. Just running her eyes over his body had hers responding. Even with the bandage covering half of his shoulder and arm, he was pure sex.

Everything about him was hard and toned. Every inch of his body was perfection.

His eyes met hers as she slid down onto him. Her thighs wrapped around his hips and she knew there was no going back. She still feared some of the horrible things she'd seen in her visions, but for now, she would take this moment. Take what she could and hold onto it for the rest of her life. No matter how short it was.

His hands went to her hips, his nails digging softly into her skin, holding her down on him. Then he nudged her to move and she obliged, moving slowly at first, then faster and faster until she felt herself once more near the edge.

Her eyes met his and she knew he, too, was moments away from release.

Her hand sought his, their fingers tangled together. She felt something shift deep inside her chest. A power that hadn't been there before. Leaning down, she placed her lips gently on his as they both jumped off the ledge together.

Ten minutes later, she stood in the shower playing over the scene in her mind.

She wasn't feeling guilty yet, but she was close. After all, she'd technically only met the guy yesterday. And cue the guilt.

Shoving her head under the water, she decided to drown those feelings.

She turned around when she felt cold air hit her. Deciding to hide her doubts for now, she turned towards him. Her eyes met his and a slow smile formed on her lips.

"You're not supposed to get that wet," she said, glancing down at his arm.

His eyes narrowed as he looked down at the white bandage covering his upper arm and shoulder.

She was shocked when he turned pale white and slid to the floor of the shower. He was too heavy for her to stop his fall, but she did shield his head from hitting the tile as she screamed his name over and over again.

Reaching up, she shut off the water, which was hitting his face full on. Her hands shook when she reached for a towel and slid it under his head.

Racing into the other room, she pulled on a

robe and dialed Xtina's number.

"Help," she said when someone answered the phone. It didn't even register who it was, only that she needed help. "Ethan's passed out in the shower." She tossed the phone on the bed, knowing that someone would be there soon. Then she went back into the shower and covered Ethan with a towel, knowing that he wouldn't appreciate everyone getting a show.

She slapped his face lightly several times, but didn't get a response. His skin was too pale, too colorless.

Tears flowed from her eyes as she called his name over and over until she heard the front door open.

"Brea?" It was Mike who rushed into the bathroom, hobbling on his good leg without a cane.

"He just passed out. Like last night," she said, shifting aside so Mike could squeeze into the shower.

"Damn," he said, shaking his brother. "Better call..." She was pretty sure he was about to say Jacob, but Ethan moaned.

"Shit," he said, pushing Mike away. "Who invited you?"

Mike chuckled, but Brea could see the worry behind his eyes. "Any time you decide to take a swan dive in the shower, I'll be here."

Brea pushed against Ethan's shoulder, keeping him from standing up. "You passed out."

"Yeah?" His eyes met hers and she could

tell he was masking his pain for his brother's benefit. "You can go." He looked over at Mike.

"Nope, not until you're back in bed." Mike stood up and leaned on the bathroom countertop.

"Where's your cane?" Ethan said as she helped him up.

"Don't need it anymore," he said, just as Xtina rushed in.

"Is he...?" She released a sigh. "Good." She handed Mike his cane. "You forgot this."

Ethan chuckled as he walked by his brother.

"Shut up," Mike said, using his cane to follow them back into the bedroom. "What the hell were you doing taking a shower anyway?"

Ethan glared at Mike. "A guy's gotta get clean somehow."

Mike's eyes moved over to Brea. She was pretty sure her face turned bright red, since it was obvious she'd been in the shower too.

"Right," Mike said, smiling. "Well, we'll leave you two...alone."

"Are you sure you're okay?" Xtina asked.

"Yeah, just bruised my ego," he said as they left. "And possibly my ass," he said when he sat on the side of the bed.

"Serves you right. What were you thinking?"

His smile was fast. "Do you really want to know?"

She groaned and rolled her eyes. "You could have waited until I was out."

He reached up and brought her closer to

him. "Waiting isn't in my vocabulary." He drew her down until their lips met.

"Why did you pass out? Maybe you need some food?"

"I could go for some food," he said after his stomach growled. But there was something else behind his eyes. Something she knew he wasn't telling her.

"How about I change your bandage again and then make us some breakfast."

He reached up and took her hand. "We could go into town for some food."

Since she was officially out of a job, she had to think about her bank account. So far, she'd been eating what food was left at Mike's place, in hopes that whatever was going on would fix itself before she ran out.

She bit her bottom lip, and Ethan rubbed his finger over her lips. "Why the worry?"

She sat down next to him and started removing his soaked bandages. "It's nothing."

His finger pushed her chin up until she was looking at him. "Brea? After last night and this morning, you can tell me anything. What's wrong?"

She sighed. "I'm sort of out of a job at the moment."

The corners of his lips turned up. "I'll buy."

She closed her eyes. "I'm not asking for charity."

"Honey, you just saved my ass for the second time since I've met you. I think I owe you that much."

Her throat threatened to close, so she just nodded. "I'll get you fresh bandages." She got up and walked into the bathroom.

Chapter Ten

*E*than chose to believe that it was the serious lack of food in his system instead of the weird déjà vu vibe he'd gotten that had caused him to pass out. He was pretty sure he'd dreamed the shower scene for the past few months. Had she had the same dreams? Would she think that he'd slept with her because he'd been dreaming about her for months?

He cringed inwardly at what she'd do. Women tended not to like it when the guy they were sleeping with ended up crazy.

Sure, they'd talked about *seeing* one another before they'd actually met. But that didn't mean he had to tell her that each dream had been X-rated. Or that she'd been turning him on since long before he ever laid eyes on her.

"Here we are." She stopped in front of the small café. He'd eaten here a few times when he'd stayed with Mike last year.

"Are you sure you're feeling up to this?"

"Yeah." He reached over and took her hand. "I'm sorry I scared you."

He still saw the worry behind her eyes. She nodded her head. "Wait until I come around. I don't want you taking another face plant. Your meds say it causes dizziness," she warned.

He would have argued with her, but she moved too fast. He felt like a freaking girl. Letting her open his door took a lot of points from his manhood score.

They walked into the diner, where an older woman waved them to take any of the free tables. Ethan followed Brea to a booth near the back and sat across from her.

"I'm starved," he admitted when his stomach growled.

"You should be. You only ate half of a slice of pizza last night." She frowned over at him.

"I didn't think anyone was paying attention."

"Everyone is worried about you." She reached across the table and took his hand.

"Yeah, I guess I'm not used to the attention," he admitted as the waitress walked towards them.

"So, you are still in town." The older woman smiled at Brea. "I thought you'd gone home."

"No." Brea smiled up at her. "Just to collect a few things. I'm staying at Mike's place. This is…"

"Ethan." Clara smiled over at him. "I know.

I heard about what happened to you." She frowned slightly as her eyes ran over his shoulder. "Breakfast is on the house for anyone who's willing to get themselves shot up giving us our freedom." She winked at him.

"Thank you." He smiled at the woman and they ordered.

"So, do you want to tell me the real reason you passed out?" she said after they were alone again.

He took a drink of his water. "Low blood sugar." She shook her head and leaned her elbows on the table. "The meds." Again, she shook her head, and this time her eyes narrowed.

"Ethan, like you said, after last night and this morning, you can tell me anything."

He hated having his words come back to him, but she was right. He couldn't keep something like this a secret, especially after she'd told him that she'd teleported. That one still got him. It was hard to wrap his mind around. He'd heard of people sleepwalking, but hadn't heard of anyone doing so when they were awake. He'd planned on doing some research on it, when he could. She seemed like a perfectly reasonable woman. Hell, he couldn't explain his visions of her either.

She sat across from him, her silver eyes glued to him.

"You're not going to believe anything I say."

"Try me." She crossed her arms over her

chest and he felt his desire for her spike.

Closing his eyes, he leaned closer. "I had a... déjà vu moment." Her eyebrows rose slightly, but she remained silent. "I'd had dreams." He shook his head. "Visions of this morning. Before."

"Which part?" she asked.

"When I walked into the shower and you turned around." He sighed and ran his hand through his hair, wishing he could pull it out. How frustrating all this was becoming. Not only was he weak as a baby, but now he kept passing out like one of those fainting goats he'd seen in a video.

She was frowning back at him. "Is that why you passed out? Did you... feel anything strange?"

He shook his head and took another drink of his water. The pills made him thirsty, and he wasn't surprised that Clara had to top off his water twice before delivering their food.

"Okay," Brea said between bites. "So, you've had visions of that moment. Any others?"

He felt the room heat and he avoided looking in her direction.

"I'll take that as a yes." She chuckled. "Don't worry, I have too."

His eyes finally met hers. "You'll have to tell..."

She broke in. "Not until you tell me first." She smiled and laughed. He liked the rich sound and couldn't stop himself from smiling back at her.

"Fair enough." He glanced around. "But, let's save that for some time when we're alone."

She nodded, "Any other... visions? One's we can talk about now?"

He thought about it. "There's the field."

Her face went a little pale and her hand stilled as she reached for her water glass. "A field?"

He nodded. "We're walking, hand in hand." He saw her relax. "Then it starts raining and we rush into a house." He shook his head remembering almost every detail about the two-story home he'd seen in his dream. "It's fuzzy, but there's someone else there. Someone we both love." His eyes met hers. He knew he was being vague, but he remembered holding a small bundle and didn't want to scare her by telling her that he was holding their child in his arms.

"Okay, I haven't seen that one."

"Tell me one of yours." He pushed his empty plate aside and thought about ordering a slice of pie or, better yet, one of those large blueberry muffins he'd seen. Having his appetite back was a good sign, right?

She frowned and he could tell she was thinking about it. "There's the tunnel," she said after a while.

"Tunnel?" He'd never dreamed of a tunnel before. "What tunnel?"

She shrugged. "I'm not sure. I've only dreamed about it once."

"Dreamed or daydreamed?"

She relaxed even more. "So, you've had these... visions when you're awake too?"

He nodded. "Sometimes they block out everything around you." When she nodded in agreement, he continued. "It's like time stops, though. Minutes pass in the vision, but in real time, it's only seconds."

"Yes, at first I thought I'd traveled." She leaned forward and lowered her voice. "But, no one around me seemed to notice."

He reached across the table and took her hand. No matter what happened, at least someone else was experiencing the same thing as him.

"Well, isn't this cozy," someone said, breaking into his thoughts.

***

Brea glanced up and jerked her hand from Ethan's.

"Drew? What are you doing here?" She frowned up at him.

"Well, I was checking in on you and your story." His eyes moved over to Ethan. "It looks like I've found the reason it's taking you so long." His voice had changed slightly with the sarcasm.

He sat next to her without asking, causing her to move over until her shoulders were pushed up against the wall.

"I'm Drew Debris." Drew held out his hand towards Ethan. "Breanna's boss and boyfriend." He glanced over at her and winked.

"Ex," she jumped in before Ethan could even blink. "Ex-boyfriend." She glared over at Drew. "Ex of several months. Several long months."

"Yes, and boss of almost two weeks."

"I thought you were in between jobs?" Ethan asked, not missing a beat.

"I am." She smiled at him, causing Drew to shift in his seat. Her shoulders straightened.

"I didn't know you were looking," Drew said, turning towards her.

"Well, what did you expect? That I would stick around without a real commitment? You do know I was up for head anchor before you came along." She tilted her head and raised her chin. "I got that far on my own merit because I'm that good at what I do."

Ethan stood up, then raised his eyebrows. "We were just leaving." He waited until Drew got the hint to let her out. "I'm sure you'll have plenty of time to talk to Brea when she wants to set time aside. Maybe you can schedule something."

Brea hid a smile by shifting out of the booth.

"Leaving so soon?" Clara walked over.

Ethan's eyes moved to Drew. "Yeah, we have some… research to do, but maybe you can pack up one of those muffins to go?" He nodded to the glass jar by the register.

"I have something even better," Clara said and disappeared.

Ethan took her hand and they walked up to the cash register together.

"I baked these myself. Cheesecake bites," Clara whispered. "Been trying to get my boss to sell them here. Let me know what you think." She handed a covered plate to Brea. "If you like them, next time you're in, let Bobby know." She nodded to the older woman standing behind the counter taking someone's order.

"Thanks, how much do…"

"Remember, it's on the house." Clara winked. "Thanks for sticking up for our rights. And next time, duck."

Ethan chuckled and nodded. "That I can do."

When they walked out of the diner, she wasn't surprised when Drew followed them.

"Breanna?" He pulled her to a stop, but a low growl from Ethan made him drop his hand. "Maybe we can meet later?"

She sighed. No matter what she said, she still needed and wanted this job. At least until she could return home and find another one.

"How about meeting around two?" she said, gauging her time.

He nodded. "I'm staying at the hotel off the highway." She held in a chuckle, knowing that he was probably stuck in the same room she'd been in and that it was far below what he was used to. "Why don't we meet there?"

"We'll meet at the library," she said firmly. "It's just down the street." She turned without giving him time to respond and walked away, holding Ethan's hand in her own.

"You handled that well," Ethan said, after they were in the car and heading out of town.

"You think?" She sighed and glanced over at him. "The guy's an ass. Cheated on me every chance he could get." She no longer felt angry, just frustrated at herself for wasting so much time with the jerk.

"Did you love him?" Ethan asked, causing her to swerve slightly.

"No!" She laughed. "Far from it."

"Good." He reached for her hand. "I don't cheat."

She smiled. "I figured you weren't the kind."

"So, do you want to tell me about your work?"

"Not really." She glanced at him, then sighed. "I'm doing an article on the cult that attacked your brother and Xtina," she said, getting into the car. "Drew took over as my boss a few weeks back, fired everyone except a few. He still hasn't made up his mind about me."

He reached over and took her hand.

"Do you want me to come with you?" he asked as they drove into the driveway.

"No." She thought of her project and cringed inwardly. What would Ethan say about her writing a paper to expose his brother's fiancée as a fraud? "I can handle Drew. Besides, I need to do this." She parked and turned off the car. "And you need your rest."

He rolled his eyes, then lowered his voice as his eyes met hers. "I rest better when you're lying beside me." He brushed a fingertip down her chin then slowly over her bottom lip.

"I thought—" Suddenly there was a knock on her window, causing her to jump.

Jacob stood outside of her car, frowning down at them.

"Sorry," he said, opening her door. "I didn't want to interrupt... anything." Jacob's eyes moved to Ethan.

Ethan crawled out of the car, holding the tray of treats. "You aren't. What's up?"

"I heard about your fall." His eyes stuck on Ethan. "You okay?"

"Yeah, sure." Ethan shut the car door and walked around.

"I..." Jacob took a breath. "I was hoping we could talk."

She walked over to Ethan and took the container. "I'll take these inside and get ready for my meeting." She disappeared quickly, not giving Ethan a chance to back down.

Chapter Eleven

Ethan watched Brea rush into the house and almost laughed at how fast she'd left him with...his brother.

He started to say, "I need a beer," but then he remembered his medicine and how early it was. "Let's go up on the porch." He nodded to the chairs he and his brother had made last time he'd visited. Even though it was chilly out, the fresh air would do him good.

Jacob was wearing street clothes, which told him that he was off duty. He sat across from him, rubbing his hands on his knees.

"So?" he said after a moment of awkward silence.

"So," Jacob repeated. "I need your help with something."

Ethan sighed. What else did he have to do besides sit around and be bored as he healed? "Shoot."

"It's about Jess." Jacob pulled out a piece of paper. "More to the point, her parents." He handed him the paper. "I would do it myself, but…" He ran his hand through his hair. "If Jess ever found out."

The look in the man's eyes told Ethan that the cop was very worried what a hundred-pound woman would do to him if she found out he was looking for her folks.

"My…our brother is better at this sort of thing. He is a PI of sorts."

"Yeah, but he's got his hands full at the moment."

He glanced over what info Jacob had found so far. Which wasn't a lot. "Why are you so concerned about finding them?"

"Jess doesn't think they have anything to do with all this, but…" He paused and looked like he wanted to say more, but instead he shrugged.

"Yeah, sure," he said after a moment. "I'll see what I can come up with. Have you heard anything more on the group that kidnapped Xtina and shot Mike?"

"The Humanist Society? The one's that survived that night have been moved to the state facility in Reidsville until their trial."

"How soon will that be?"

Jacob laughed. "Not soon enough. Their leader, William…"

"Yeah, Mike told me about him." Ethan sighed, thankful that his brother had taken care of the bastard himself.

"Well, he sure left a mark on this town." He

was pretty sure he saw Jacob shiver. "The people in Hidden Creek have been super vigilant since then. No strangers can drive through town without getting questioned."

"Gotta love small towns."

"Actually, we've had so many tips, we've been crazy busy."

Ethan folded the paper and put it in his pocket as Brea walked out with some pills and a glass of water.

"Time for these." She handed another glass to Jacob after making sure he swallowed the two pills. "Sorry, we didn't have any tea."

Jacob held up the water and smiled. "Water's fine."

"So, how about the Schmitt's case?" Brea asked as she sat next to him.

Ethan had heard about it, the one thing his parents had mentioned to him.

"What about it?" Jacob asked.

"Any new info on that case?" she asked and Ethan could tell that she was in full reporter mode, something he'd never seen before. If he had to be honest, it was turning him on.

"Like I told you at the station, the boyfriend confessed and pointed at the wife, but so far Mrs. Schmitt hasn't squealed."

"Is she still claiming Xtina was in on it?"

Ethan sat up a little. He hadn't heard that part of the story. "What?"

Jacob glanced over at him. "Yeah, she's claiming it was Xtina's fault. That she somehow took control of her. Bewitched her." He rolled his eyes and laughed.

"Seriously?" Ethan leaned forward. "There's no way that kind of..." He stopped himself as he remembered all the things Brea had admitted to him. Hell, if someone could believe they could teleport, then why not believe a witch could control someone.

"Yeah, right." Jacob took another sip of his water. "I mean, there's a lot of crazy shit that's been going on lately, but that..." He shook his head. "Nope. That's where I think the line is crossed. Being able to control someone else."

Ethan laughed, but something deep in his gut twisted. "Listen, I think I'm going to lay down for a while." He nodded towards his shoulder.

Jacob set his glass down on the end table. "Sure. I heard about what happened with you. We didn't get a chance to talk much last time, but I wanted to say I appreciate your service." He reached out for Ethan's left hand.

When Ethan shook it, a shock traveled up his arm.

Suddenly, he was standing at the base of a silo. Jacob, Mike, Xtina, and Jess were all standing in a circle, and the heavy doors were open as the full moon shone down on them all.

He glanced around, looking for Brea, but she wasn't there.

Then there was a bright flash, and suddenly, she was there, standing in the middle of the five of them. Her silver eyes went directly to his.

"I love you," she said. Something told him that it wasn't the first time she'd said it to him, but it was the most important.

They all lifted their arms as Jess started chanting something in a different language.

Then another woman appeared and Brea stepped towards him. He broke the connection and reached for her, but when he did, she disappeared quickly, fading back into the darkness.

Someone screamed and when he glanced up, a fireball was falling from the sky, directly towards them.

The vision disappeared when Jacob dropped his hand and took a step back.

"Whoa," Jacob said, shaking his head. "What the hell."

"Ethan?" Brea reached over and took his arm. "Are you okay?"

"Yeah, just freaking peachy keen." He stood up and walked into the house without another word, leaving Jacob and Brea outside.

He hated being weak. Hated that his body couldn't stay up with his mind. Hated the damn visions that were ruining his life. Hell, he didn't know what half of them meant.

He'd tried to go without the pills and had ended up face down, so he was trying it with the pills and ended up weak as a baby.

He was getting tired of this shit.

***

Ethan had laid down on the bed in the other room after Jacob had left. She sat at the kitchen

123

table, getting her files together for her meeting with Drew. She had so many notes on her life, on what was happening to her, that she didn't know where to begin.

The information she had on Xtina had easily tripled in the past few days. She had files on each of them: Xtina, Mike, Jess, Jacob, and Ethan.

There was so much information she didn't want Drew to get his hands on, so she dumped those files into a folder on her USB memory stick.

She knew Drew wasn't going to let up until he had what she had. After all, why would he drive over an hour and stay in a hole-in-a-wall hotel. He was here for more than just the story and that made her skin crawl.

She shut her laptop and tucked the USB drive into the pocket of her bag with her tablet. A movement caught her eye across the room. Thinking it was Ethan, she glanced over and held in a scream.

There, hovering a few feet away, was her aunt. It took a moment for her heart to start beating again. She felt shivers race over her skin.

Then she remembered how Xtina and Mike had told her that they had been seeing Misty and her brain clicked.

"Aunt Misty?" Her aunt turned towards her, her silver eyes meeting her own. "What do you want?" Her aunt turned towards the bedroom and then back towards her. A sad look crossed her eyes before she disappeared.

Brea let out the breath she'd been holding. What the hell was that?

Debating whether to wake Ethan up and tell him what had just happened, she glanced down at her watch and realized she didn't have time. Grabbing her coat, she hoisted her bag over her shoulder and left. She'd have to tell Ethan about her encounter later.

What did it mean, her aunt showing up again? Did it mean anything? So many questions raced through her mind.

By the time she got to town, she was feeling a little better. She parked in front of the library and gauged she was about five minutes early. She saw Drew standing out front.

She knew his M.O. He'd tried to get her back to his hotel by smooth talking her. That was not going to happen again. Ever.

"Hello, Drew." She walked past him and towards the front door, but his hand on her arm stopped her.

"Hang on a moment," Drew said, pulling her close. "Why the rush? I thought maybe we could…"

"Drew," she warned, leaning closer, "either you come into the library and we have a civil conversation, employee to boss, or I get back in the car and start looking for someone else who's interested in the story." She jerked her arm free and walked past him, happy to note that he was close on her heels. She was proud that she'd taken the first step in taking back her future.

That was until she walked into the library and found herself surrounded by over two dozen screaming kids.

"Sorry," the librarian standing behind the counter said, looking overly apologetic. "It's the fourth Tuesday in the month." she said before returning her eyes to the computer screen, like Brea was supposed to know what that meant.

"Maybe we can find a quiet corner?" she suggested, walking towards the back of the library. She did not want to take him to the basement to be alone and was thankful when she found a quiet reading room near the back.

"Brea, this is ridiculous," Drew said, walking directly to her and taking her shoulders. "Why can't we talk this out."

She felt her entire body tense. "What? The fact that you're holding my career over my head to get me in bed again?"

His eyes narrowed and she realized she'd guessed the game he was playing correctly. She jerked her shoulders free and walked over to sit behind the table.

"Now, if you don't mind, I'd like to go over our choices."

He crossed his arms over his chest and glared at her. "From where I'm standing, I can see only one path."

"Which would be?" She had a sinking feeling in her gut.

He took his time and walked over to sit across from her, settling in the chair like he had all the time in the world.

"Write this piece and come home. You'll keep your position"—his eyes ran over her face slowly and she felt a shiver rush through her—"as long as you give me another chance."

"You're right, Drew." She stood up slowly as anger vibrated deep inside her. She swung her bag to her shoulder. "There is only one way for this to work. I write my piece"—she took a step towards the door—"and sell it to the highest bidder."

She didn't even get to the door before Drew had her arm, his fingers digging into her flesh above her elbow.

"Easy," he said softly, his other hand going to her shoulders. "Why all the pent-up anger towards me? I thought we left things at a good place."

She rolled her eyes, then pushed him back. She was a little surprised when he stepped away easily.

"Is your new boy toy not pleasing you?" he said, crossing his arms over his chest.

"You're such an ass."

"Yeah, so I've been told." He glanced at her bag, then turned towards her again. "Listen, can we start over?" She sighed and nodded. "So, what *do* you have?"

She thought about her hidden files and decided to stick to her plan of giving him something so he'd leave and get off her back.

She pulled out her tablet and flipped it open, opening the files she'd prepared just for him.

"On Xtina? Not much. Other than she's…"

"Xtina? You mean, her…" He sat again and

pointed to a picture on her screen. "Christina Warren?"

"Yes." She flipped to her notes. "I've been staying at the place across from her and have gotten close to her. But so far, all I've learned is that she appears legit."

"Legit?" He laughed. "Yeah, right." He leaned back. "What's gotten into you?" he said after a moment.

"You want what I have or not?" she asked.

"Email it to me." He reached for her hand, which she moved out of his reach.

"Is that why you drove all the way to Hidden Creek? Why you're holed up in what has to be the worst hotel imaginable?" She shut her tablet. "For me to email what I have to you?"

He chuckled. "Let's just say I'm personally invested in this one."

"Why?" She could tell he was holding something back, but couldn't see his angle.

When he leaned forward and brushed a finger across her knuckles, she frowned over at him.

"Seriously?" She laughed and gathered her stuff up for the second time. "Don't you think that ship has sailed?"

"Listen, Brea, I know I've made mistakes in the past."

Her chuckle stopped him. "You call cheating on me several times… a mistake?"

"Yeah." He smiled slightly, then shifted towards her and his smile fell away. "But in the last few months, I've done some personal growing.

I realize I was wrong. I'm sorry."

It was funny, looking into his eyes, she could see that he really meant it.

"Too late," she said softly. "Listen, there might have been a time..." She shook her head. "Well, no, actually not after I found out. I appreciate your honesty and your apology, but I'm not the kind of woman who can forgive and forget that easily."

She shoved her tablet into her bag and threw it over her shoulder. "Go home, Drew. I'll send you what I have." She walked to the door and opened it.

"Brea." She glanced over her shoulder at him. "Regardless of what happens, your spot at the station will be there."

She tilted her head and smiled. "Thanks, Drew."

The entire drive home, she was almost in shock. What had caused Drew to act that way? There was some serious crazy stuff going on lately. And it was her job to figure it out, wrap it up with a freaking bow, and hand it over to Drew.

Maybe that was his angle? Get the story, then cut her lose? She knew she wasn't the only journalist sniffing around town. She'd seen the crew for WSUN in the coffee shop just that morning when they'd been at the diner.

If they were in town, too, that meant Drew was really getting itchy to get his hands on the story. She doubted he'd be leaving town anytime soon, but she hoped.

When she pulled into the drive, the rain started, the kind of rain that came down in buckets. Big ones. She grabbed her umbrella and ran through the mud only to bump into Jess on the porch.

"Hey," Jess said, frowning at her.

"Sorry, I didn't see you." Brea shook her umbrella off.

"It's okay, I was just... waiting for you. I knocked, but..." Jess frowned at her. Her fingers bunched in front of her. There were dark circles under her eyes and she looked like she'd dressed in a hurry. She nodded towards the chairs on the front porch, then walked over and sat down. Brea followed her and sat across from her, setting her bag on the chair beside her.

"Ethan's probably still sleeping." Worry flooded her mind, but she didn't want Jess to see it.

"Listen, I heard about... your deal." Her eyebrows went up. "From Xtina. She said that you show up in places..."

"Yeah." She shook her head. "I still can't believe it myself."

"I've seen it," Jess said, and for the first time, Brea realized the woman looked scared.

"Are you okay?" she asked, leaning forward.

"Yeah." Jess rolled her shoulders and relaxed slightly. "I've seen..."—she closed her eyes and sighed—"something, my whole life, but it didn't make sense until Xtina told me what you could do."

"What have you seen?"

She shook her head. "It's not important at the moment. Can you control it?"

"Control?" She laughed and shook her head.

"Well, you've got to work on it." Jess sat forward. "You have to learn how to control it."

"How? If you have any clue as to what I can do…"

"Hi," Ethan's voice came from the doorway, causing both women to jump.

"You're awake." Brea stood and walked over to him. She noticed that his coloring was much better than it had been earlier. The dark circles under his eyes were gone and his dark eyes looked a lot clearer.

"Everything okay?" He let Brea lead him to a chair.

"Yes." It was Jess that spoke. "We were just having a chat."

"About?" Ethan asked Brea.

"Brea's talents," Jess supplied before she could stop her.

"Talents." Brea laughed. Right, talents.

"Her abilities," Jess said after Ethan looked at them blankly. "Teleportation."

His eyes moved to Brea. "And?"

"She needs to learn to control it," Jess said, looking even more agitated. "Fast."

"Why?" Ethan asked, beating her to the punch line.

Jess glanced over at the big house across the field. "Something's coming."

Chapter Twelve

Ethan felt better. Much better. Like he'd taken some sort of wonder pill. He'd woken up fresh with his mind clear. He felt great. Well, except for the nagging pain in his shoulder and arm. He might even be able to go a full twelve hours without falling over.

The rain was coming down pretty hard now. The sound of it had woken him.

When he'd walked out onto the porch, Brea looked like she'd been struck by lightning.

Then Jess had thrown a spooky wrench in the evening.

"Something's coming," Jess said, as she looked over at the big house across the field.

"How does she control it?" Ethan asked, looking between them.

"Like, I should know," Jess said, turning

back around.

The sky had grown dark, very dark, due to the cloud coverage. The weather didn't look like it was going to let up anytime soon.

"Well, any clues?" Brea asked.

"Nope, none so far. All I know is that something bad is coming."

"Okay," he said, running his hands through his hair. "Any clue when?"

"Full moon," Brea and Jess said at the same time.

"Okay, so, about two weeks from now?"

"No," Brea said. "The hunter's moon."

"Hunter's moon?" He didn't know much about the moon phases.

"Yeah, the next one is in October. Only appears once every four years."

"This October?" He got a nod. "That's next month."

"Yup," Jess said, crossing her arms over her chest. Her phone beeped and she glanced down at it. "Listen, I've got to go." She moved towards the stairs.

"Here." Brea handed her an umbrella. "There's more inside."

Jess took the umbrella. "Work with her," Jess said before turning and leaving.

"Okay, so how do you want to do this thing?" he asked when they were alone.

She surprised him by laughing. "What I want is a drink." She got up and disappeared into the house.

He followed her, desperately wishing for a

beer but unsure all the pills were out of his system yet.

Brea went into the kitchen and poured herself some wine. She paused, then poured herself some more, shrugging at him.

"It's been one of those days." She set the bottle down and swallowed a drink.

"So, how *did* the meeting go?" he asked, sitting down on a bar stool.

She laughed. "Not as crazy as what we were just talking about out there." She nodded towards the front door.

"Yeah, so what do you make of all that?" He took a bottle of water from the fridge.

"I'm not sure how she thinks I can learn to control... my talent."

"Have you tried?" he asked, taking a drink.

"Yes." She sat down on the sofa.

He followed her. "And?"

"And, nothing ever happened. Xtina even offered to help, but nothing." She shrugged.

"When was the last time you..."

"Transported?" she supplied.

"Yeah."

"The night I showed up in Hidden Creek. The night you got hurt."

"Yeah, Mike told me that it was... how did he put it... a shared experience."

"Was that the time you lost time?"

She nodded. "Apparently a few days."

"And it felt like no time had passed?"

"Yup, one minute I had just walked into my

apartment in Atlanta, and the next I'm standing on Xtina's front porch, my skin tingling."

He reached across the bar and touched her hand. "We'll figure this out."

"Yeah." She rolled her eyes. "How about I make us some dinner?"

For the next few minutes, he sat at the bar and watched her cook. He laughed when he noticed she was cooking breakfast.

"Is that French toast?"

"Yeah, I like breakfast for dinner when I'm stressed," she said, flipping a piece of toast.

"Hey, no argument from me. I love French toast."

She set a plate in front of him and he felt his mouth water at the look she gave him across the bar.

"Looks like you got some rest," she said, sitting next to him.

"Yeah, I feel like a new man." He reached over and took her hand in his. "I know things have been... rushed."

She smiled and took a sip of her orange juice.

"But with the dreams we've both had, I can't help feeling like we're moving too slow."

Her smile fell away and her eyes met his.

"Ethan, sometimes..." She shook her head and squeezed his hand, then dropped it. "Sometimes I'm not even sure what is real or dream anymore."

"Yeah, I get that. When I was over there"—his mind turned to his last mission—"I was pretty sure that line was so blurred, I was going to screw things up. Actually, it's probably the reason for this." He held up his shoulder.

"What do you mean?" She shifted slightly towards him.

"I was so far gone in fantasizing about some sexy blonde with eyes like the moon that I didn't see the sniper."

***

Brea's heart fluttered in her chest and she couldn't stop from smiling as she finished her food.

"Did it hurt?" she asked as she put the last dish into the dishwasher.

"What?" he asked, caging her against the countertop. His hand moved over her hip, holding her close.

"That." She ran her finger over his bandage, enjoying how wonderful he felt up against her.

"It only really hurts when I move." He smiled at her and she felt her knees weaken.

"Then you'd better not move." She leaned up and placed a kiss on his lips. She took a step and nudged him again until his back was against the countertop, her lips never leaving his.

His eyes stayed on hers as she unbuttoned his shirt button by button.

When she nudged the cotton over his shoulders, he moved slightly and she saw the pain cross his eyes briefly.

"You're not supposed to move." She

glanced at him and tossed his shirt away. "Remember?"

His smile returned. "I'm at your command," he said softly.

Her eyes stayed locked with his as she ran her fingers over his impressive chest and arms. "This is very impressive."

She leaned down and ran kisses over every spot her fingers had just been. She heard him hiss, but when she glanced up, a smile played on his lips.

"So you mean to torture me?" He chuckled and she felt it rumble in his chest. "Maybe we should move to..." He nodded towards the back of the house.

"No, I kind of like it here." She pushed him back again until he sat on the edge of the countertop.

She stepped between his legs, holding him close and pulled his head down to her as she kissed him over and over. She felt the urge grow so fast in her.

When his fingers moved up to nudge her shirt aside, she playfully slapped his hand.

"Help me out here," he said, nodding towards her shoulder.

She took a step back, then slowly removed her shirt.

She never, in a million years, would have believed she would be stripping for anyone. Especially someone she'd met only a day ago.

But, she had to admit, it was amazingly liberating. She peeled off every scrap of clothing, but stopped when she stood in the kitchen in only her matching panties and bra.

His eyes ate her up, watching every move she made. When her finger dipped under the strap of her bra, his lips curled up. But instead of dropping the rest of her clothes, she stepped forward and reached out to run her finger over the top of his jeans.

His eyes closed and he rolled his head back and groaned with pleasure when her hand roamed over his hardness.

"You like this?"

"My god!" he said. "Yes."

She opened the button on his jeans, then slowly slid his zipper down. When she nudged the jeans over his hips, her breath caught at his beauty.

Biting her bottom lip, she smiled up at him. "Step out." She helped him step out of his jeans. "Now the fun begins."

When her lips covered his, she felt her entire body respond as she touched him everywhere.

"Brea," he said between heavy breaths, "let me..."

She chuckled, stopping him. "Soon." She pushed his boxers down his legs and wrapped her hand around his arousal. She heard his breath hitch as he sucked in a breath.

"I can't help but feeling empowered." She smiled as she moved her hand over him. "Like a genie, finally out of my bottle."

He growled, actually growled, as his dark

eyes burned into her.

Then, before she could respond, her back was up against the fridge. In one quick swipe, her panties were ripped away from her as his fingers cupped her.

A scream escaped her lips, just before he covered them with a tender kiss. There was so much power here. Between them. She felt it growing, building, until her body arched to take him in.

Even then, she wasn't satisfied and begged for more.

"Ethan," she begged, "I need…"

"What, say it. Say it," he moaned as his lips traveled over the hollow spot between her neck and her shoulder.

"You," she uttered softly. "I need you inside me. Now." Her nails dug into his hips as she wrapped a leg around him.

Then he was spinning her around once again. With his good arm, he hoisted her up easily until she sat on the edge of the bar. His thighs nudged her legs wider until he stood between them. She felt him just outside her and closed her eyes on a moan.

"Yes."

"Look at me," he said, next to her lips. "I want to see your eyes change as I enter you."

Her eyes slid open as he took her in one quick motion.

She was completely destroyed. Her heart ached, actually ached as she watched pleasure spread on his face.

She'd never felt anything as powerful as the release he'd given her. Somehow, she knew he was feeling the same thing. His entire body jolted with it, and when they both started to relax after, she felt warmth spread straight to her heart.

When he smiled at her, she knew there was no way to fight her feelings anymore.

"Why is it I feel like we've known each other forever?" she asked as he stepped back and handed her his shirt.

She smiled as she pulled it on and buttoned a few buttons, covering herself.

"Because we have." He pulled up his jeans with his good hand, then grunted when he tried to use his bad arm to help. "In a way."

"Yeah, our visions." She rolled her eyes. "Okay, how about we try something?"

His laughter stopped her from finishing putting on her jeans. "What?"

"Didn't we just *try* something?" His eyebrows wiggled. "I'm game, though I might need a minute."

She chuckled. "Later. For now, how about we play twenty questions?"

"Sounds fun. How about some popcorn?" he asked, walking over to the cupboard.

"You start a fire; I'll make the popcorn." She took the box of microwave stuff from him. "It's gotten chilly in here."

Ten minutes later, they sat in front of the fireplace with a large bowl of popcorn and two root beers, asking each other any questions they could come up with.

She found that they had the same favorite color, red. The same favorite number, 27. And, even odder, the same favorite shape, a pyramid.

"I've always wanted to go to Egypt," she admitted.

"I did too, until I had a mission there." He shook his head. "Let's just say, it's not like you see in the photos."

"Yeah," she sighed. "If only you could go back in time." She tucked her legs underneath her and smiled when he handed her the blanket from the back of the sofa.

"It's normally not this cold this early."

"I guess hurricane season brought a bunch of cold winds." He tossed a few more logs on the fire. The rain was still coming down, and every now and then, lightning would flood the room with light.

"I don't mind the cold. My father used to take me to Colorado every Christmas. We'd spend a week skiing and playing in the snow." She remembered all the fun they would have together. "But, after I graduated, our trips stopped."

"What about your mother?"

Sadness still overtook her when she thought about the woman who'd given birth to her. "She died, giving birth to me."

"I'm sorry." He gathered her in his arms. "So, your aunt..."

"My father and my aunt Misty were an item before my parents, something I didn't know until I saw a picture in the local paper from back then. All my dad told me was that my aunt died in a freak accident in high school. My parents married shortly after graduating and, a few years later, they had me. Then my father became a single parent." She rested her head on his good shoulder.

His arm wrapped around her shoulder and she sighed at how wonderful it felt.

"I guess we both found out some new stuff about our parents," he said.

"From what Xtina has said, it didn't sound like your parents had a choice. I can't imagine what you're going through, finding out you have a brother after all these years."

He shifted and cringed with pain.

"You need some more pills." She moved to get up, but he stopped her.

"No, I'll be fine. I just need some more rest." He pulled her back down until she rested against his chest. "I wonder why my parents didn't tell me about Jacob? Instead, they left it up to Mike."

"They're probably having a hard time with it," she suggested. "The last time I talked to my father, he wouldn't answer any questions about Misty or my mother. Come to think about it, he seemed reluctant to mention that he'd lived in Hidden Creek before."

They were silent for a while, listening to the thunder as the storm slowly moved away from them.

"What could have happened here to cause my aunt to appear like this?" she said, after a yawn.

"You've seen her?" he asked, brushing a hand down her hair.

"Twice now. Once in the hotel, the day I left… and the other…" She leaned up and looked at him. "Earlier today." She nodded towards the spot. "Right over there."

Chapter Thirteen

By the next morning, Ethan felt almost back to normal, which was odd. It was like being with Brea had somehow sped up the healing process.

He even went for a walk to the end of the road and back. The four miles would have to hold him over for now, seeing as he felt winded and tired by the time he climbed the porch stairs.

When he walked in, he smiled upon seeing Brea in the kitchen, making breakfast.

"Making dinner for breakfast?" he asked when he saw the steaks in the pan.

She chuckled and shook her head. "No, steak and eggs is breakfast."

"Right." He smiled. "You won't hear me complaining." He took a bottle of water from the fridge and drank half of it down.

"Should you be taking long walks so soon?" she asked, flipping a steak.

"Sure, I've never felt better." He smiled, and rolled his shoulders, only feeling a slight twinge when he did. "Not bad."

"So, I thought we'd swing by the library again. There's a lot of microfiche I didn't get to."

"Seriously? What do you hope to learn?"

"I don't know." She flipped the thin steaks out of the pan and onto two plates with scrambled eggs and set a plate in front of him. "I'm hoping to find something that can shed some light on what's going on. Why everything is happening. What really happened to my aunt."

He took a bite of the steak and moaned with pleasure. "Well, if you keep feeding me like this, you can count me in for anything."

Four hours later, he felt his eyeballs were going to pop out of their sockets. They had gone through stacks of small black film, reading old newspaper articles.

"I can't believe that this is how people used to do research for papers." He shook his head and flipped to another page. "Hang on." He leaned back. "Here's the article about your aunt."

Brea swung her chair towards his and read along over his shoulder.

"It says here that your aunt drowned at the lake. That her body was never found."

"Marshal Lake," she read over his shoulder. "That's a few miles out of town." She turned to him. "Up for a drive?"

Just then more thunder sounded and her shoulders slumped.

"Maybe tomorrow." He reached out and

brushed a strand of hair away from her forehead. "Don't worry, we'll figure this out."

She nodded. "Let's print a copy of this so we can take it with us."

"How about we take a break from all this, get some take-out, and rent a movie online."

She smiled. "Now you're reading my mind."

His eyes got huge and he put a finger to her temple, then his. "I see a night of good Chinese take-out, a cheesy chick flick, and all-night lovemaking." He leaned in and placed a slow, passionate kiss on her lips.

"Your powers are truly amazing." She laughed as she started gathering up her notes.

The Chinese place was closed due to a grease fire, so they grabbed a few burgers from the diner instead.

When they walked into the house, he set the take-out bag on the bar, then went and got them each a beer.

"Looks like we'll need a run into the store soon." He set the beer down in front of her and she looked at him like he had two heads.

He reached out to touch her hand, but she yanked it away and screamed.

"No!"

Her eyes turned a lighter shade of silver and she started to disappear. He stood there in complete shock as she faded.

It took him approximately two seconds to react. First, he blinked to make sure he wasn't hallucinating. Then he reached out and touched thin air.

He called Xtina, Mike, Jess, and Jacob in a panic, and by the time they arrived, he was in full denial mode.

"What the hell just happened?" he asked when he opened the door.

"Why are you asking us?" Jacob said, stepping in and scanning the room.

"One minute we were there, about to have a beer and dinner, then poof."

"Did she actually go poof?" Jess asked, causing everyone to look at her. "What?" She shrugged.

"No. She just faded." He felt sick to his stomach. "She sparkled, then I blinked and she was gone."

"Did she say anything before she... left?" Xtina asked.

"She said no. Just no." He sat down, then immediately got up and took a swig of his beer.

"So, we need to go over everything." Xtina sat down, followed by Jess. "Jess and I were talking, and we're pretty sure that her being able to control her ability plays a pretty big part in all this."

"Yeah, we talked about that some."

"Is there anything you can tell us? What was she doing before? What were you talking about?" Jacob grabbed a beer and tossed one to Mike.

"We were talking about... well, nothing really. We had just gotten back from getting food at the diner." He ran his hands through his hair.

"What were you talking about specifically?" Xtina said.

"We had been talking about finding out about her aunt drowning at the lake."

Suddenly, the air in the room sizzled.

"No!" Brea continued to say from the chair at the bar.

***

"What happened?" Brea said, staring across the room at everyone.

Ethan rushed over, tipping over his beer, and wrapped his arms around her. "Don't you ever scare me like that again."

By the way he was holding her, she knew he'd been just as scared as she was.

"You disappeared," he said, still holding her. "For almost an hour."

"An hour?" She felt her stomach roll and everything in the room spun. Next thing she knew, she was waking up on the sofa with five set of eyes looking down at her.

"Sorry." She tried to sit up, but several hands reached out and held her still.

Jess thrust a bottle of water in her face. "Drink."

She took several drinks and immediately started to feel better.

"I'm fine." She sat up, and this time everyone stood back.

"Where did you go?" It was Jess who asked.

"The lake. One minute I was there"—her eyes moved to the chair where she'd been sitting— "and the next I was standing on the edge of a lake." She looked down at her dirty shoes and closed her eyes on a groan. She had been there. This time, it wasn't a dream.

"You screamed, no," Ethan said, his hands closing around hers.

"I felt like I was going to go, but..." She shook her head. "I couldn't control it."

"You pushed my hand away." Ethan shifted when she sat up.

"I... I didn't want to drag you." She looked around at everyone. "I'm not even sure I can."

The entire room was silent and she could feel the energy building.

"I'll heat up your burgers," Jess said, breaking into the silence.

"Actually, I'm not hungry anymore. But, I could use a drink."

Jacob and Mike both shoved their beers in her face, and she laughed. "Thanks." She reached over and grabbed the bottle from Ethan and took a swallow.

"How about I run into town and grab us all some burgers and fries?" Jacob suggested. "Then we can figure out what this is all about."

"I'll go with," Jess said, moving towards the door without waiting.

By the time they returned, the entire vibe in the room had changed.

Everyone was on a mission. Even her. She'd flipped open her tablet and had taken notes on every detail she could remember as everyone talked around her.

"Okay," Mike said as everyone started eating their food. "Why don't you tell us what you saw at the lake. Did you see the entity?" He shook his head. "I mean your aunt?"

"Why did you call my aunt an entity and not a ghost?" Everyone in the room stopped eating and turned towards Mike.

"Well, there's a difference." He started to explain, then looked at Xtina. "She showed me."

Xtina set down her burger. "Your aunt isn't dead."

Everyone in the room talked at the same time, throwing questions at Xtina, who held up her hands until everyone was quiet again.

"There are differences between ghosts and your aunt. When I touch, so to speak, someone who has passed, I can't touch their minds. I get flooded with emotions—anger, fear, happiness, loneliness, and so on."

"And with my aunt?"

"There's more..." She tapped the side of her head. "So much more up there."

"Like?" Jacob asked.

"Memories," Xtina said.

Brea visibly shivered. "And ghosts... not that I'm saying they exist, but ghosts don't have memories?"

"No," both Mike and Xtina answered.

"What about the vision we had?" Jess asked. "You know, seeing her in the water?"

Mike, Jacob, Xtina, and Jess all had sour looks on.

"What's this about water?" Ethan asked as his eyes met hers.

Mike looked towards Xtina. "Before the shit hit the fan a few weeks ago, we were all sitting around, kind of like we are now."

"We were toasting to something, and wham-o," Jess added. "We all had the same vision."

"All of you?" she asked, looking around at the four of them.

"I wasn't there," Jacob said, holding up his hands.

"I wonder..." Jess said, looking down at her beer. She held it up and shrugged. "Worth a try."

One by one, everyone gathered around the coffee table and held their drinks inches from one another.

"Ready?" Xtina asked. Everyone nodded in turn, then clinked their bottles together.

Nothing happened.

"Well, that was fun," Jacob said sarcastically as he sat back down.

"There has to be a reason it worked before," Xtina said, biting her bottom lip.

"What else had we done?" Mike asked.

"Well, it was wine last time, not beer," Jess supplied.

"And they were in my mother's good crystal glasses. Remember? They shattered."

"Crystal," Jess and Xtina said at the same

time.

"Mike?" Xtina turned to him.

"Way ahead of you," he said, hobbling towards the kitchen. "I think I might have some. I bought some Dorset bar glasses at an antique shop a while back." He set one down from the cupboard and smiled. "A set of eight."

"I'll pour the wine," Jess said, pulling a bottle from the fridge.

Chapter Fourteen

The energy in the room was so high, Ethan felt the hairs on his arm rise.

"We doing this?" he asked, holding his own glass inches from everyone else's.

"What exactly are we expecting to happen?" Jacob asked.

"Something," Jess said, shrugging. "At least we're trying."

"What? To knock ourselves out again just to see a ghost?" Mike said, shaking his head.

"Well, at least it's something," Xtina said and held up her glass. "Ready?"

Everyone nodded.

"May our friendship never fail, may we always be kind, I'll post your bail, if you post mine." Jess smiled and moved her glass to everyone else's.

At the moment the six glasses connected, a flash almost blinded him as the fine crystal shattered in his hand. A strong wave of power spiked through Ethan's bones.

Suddenly, he was standing in a field. He turned and started walking towards Brea, who was standing a few feet away. As he walked towards her, she turned to him.

"You have to let me go." Her silver eyes were determined. Then suddenly she vanished, and he was left alone.

Then as fast as he'd arrived, he was pulled back to his brother's living room.

Everyone else was still gazing blankly into space.

He reached over and touched Brea's face. She felt cold, but she was breathing normally. So was everyone else, as far as he could tell.

One by one, they came back to themselves.

"That was odd," Jacob said, reaching for his beer.

"Last time everyone saw the same thing." Xtina looked around. "What did you see this time?" She turned to Jess.

"Oh no, I'm not going first." She shook her head and leaned back, crossing her arms over her chest.

Ethan didn't know Jess very well, but he was pretty sure there was no way she was going to change her mind.

"Fine, I'll go first." Xtina took a drink of her beer. "I was back in the silo." He saw her shiver as his brother reached over and took her hand in his.

"And?" Jess asked.

"I was in a different room. One I don't remember." Her eyes went to Brea. "What did you see, Mike?"

"I was back in the silo too, in the missile area. There was water in the bottom of it like before."

Jacob spoke up, "I was at the lake. That's it." He turned and looked at Jess. "You were there."

"Yeah," Jess sighed. "I was."

Ethan watched as something passed between the two of them. Then everyone turned towards him.

"I was in a field." When everyone continued to wait, he added, "The moon."

"What about it?" Jacob asked.

"It was a sliver."

"Was it waxing?" Jess asked.

"What kind of question is that?" Jacob turned to her.

She shrugged. "A normal one." She looked around. "Was it a waxing crescent or a waning crescent?"

"Who knows the difference?" he asked.

Again, everyone just looked at her until she sighed. "Which way was it cupped?" She held her hands up in two cups. "This way or that?"

"I don't remember."

Jess pulled out her phone, typed a few things, and turned it around. "This is a waxing crescent. It happens after a new moon. This is waning crescent. It happens before a new moon. We can estimate when this is going to happen."

"That one, I guess." He nodded. "To be honest, I didn't really pay attention. Brea was there, then she wasn't."

"The next waxing crescent is in two weeks," Jess said, looking down at her phone.

Everyone was silent for a while.

Then, everyone turned to Brea.

"What did you see?" Xtina asked.

"I…" She swallowed a sip of her wine, then got up and walked to the fireplace and reached towards the warmth. "I didn't see anything," she said with her back to the group.

"What does that mean?" Ethan asked, looking around the room at everyone else.

"I don't know, but…" She shook her head. "Nothing happened."

"Strange. Why would we all see something but not you?" Mike asked.

"Does any of this really make sense?" she asked and looked down at her hands.

Everyone shrugged as they looked at one another.

"I need another beer." Jacob walked to the fridge and opened it. "You're out." He looked over at Jess. "Why don't we call it?"

Everyone looked at Jess.

Xtina jumped in. "You two?" She balked. "Are together?"

"No!" Jess stood up. "He drove me here." She walked over and picked up her coat. "What?" she said to Xtina. "He was at the coffee shop."

Ethan glanced at Jacob and saw the truth in his eyes. He held in a chuckle.

"Whatever," Xtina said, smiling. "We'd better go let Rose out." She stood and helped Mike up.

After everyone left, Ethan turned towards Brea. She was still standing at the fireplace, her arms wrapped around herself.

"So," he said, setting his feet up on the coffee table, "want to tell me what you really saw?"

Her eyes moved to his. "What do you mean?"

"We may have actually only met a few days ago, but up here"—he tapped his head— "I've known you a lot longer. And you're not a very good liar."

She sat next to him and tucked her feet up under her.

"I was in the field." Her eyes met his and he thought he saw sadness behind them. "Then, I was in the tunnel."

"A tunnel?"

"Yeah." She closed her eyes and leaned her head back. "I've been there before."

"For real?"

"No, yes." She shook her head. "In a vision."

"And?" He pulled her close, seeing that she was getting frustrated.

She relaxed against his chest. "Something was off, like I wasn't supposed to be there. Like something didn't want me to be there." She shivered, so he wrapped his arms around her.

"I watched you disappear from the field," he said, running his hand over her hair.

"I saw that too. I try to fight it, like I have some sort of control over it."

"If Jess is correct, we have two weeks." He pulled her closer and brushed a kiss over her hair.

"How's your shoulder?" she asked.

"Fine." He smiled, knowing that the worst of the pain was over. "I was lucky."

She surprised him by twisting around and straddling him. She leaned in and placed a kiss on his lips, slowly running her hands over his chest. "Yes, you are."

***

Brea needed to get her mind off of what she'd seen and the best way to do that was to fill her mind and body with Ethan.

Straddling him felt so good. His hands went to her hips, and he dug his nails into her soft skin as he pulled her clothes off her slowly. When they were both naked and lying in front of the fire, she finally felt in control again.

She hovered over him, her hands sprawled on his chest.

"Ethan." She smiled down at him.

He pulled her down and ran his lips over hers.

The fire crackled as she enjoyed him. Heat spread throughout her entire system. Her eyes met his as the pleasure pulsed throughout her system.

"Let go," he said next to her ear. "Just let go." How could she deny him? She moved over him until he filled her and soon she felt herself slipping.

By morning, she was feeling a little more centered. She'd been thrown off by everything she'd seen yesterday. Learning about her aunt.

She needed a new plan of attack. Something that would help her in her research.

She planned to look over her notes again that day, maybe talk to Ethan about some of the other things she'd found out. But for now, she was going to enjoy the feel of him lying next to her.

She couldn't remember the last time she'd felt so alive. Or so connected. Even before Drew, she'd never felt this close to someone before.

She wasn't sure if she could keep herself from opening up to him about it either.

"What's on the agenda?" he asked, running a hand up her arm.

"I was thinking we could go over a few things before heading out to the lake. But first..." She leaned in and kissed him until she felt him respond to her. Then she pulled away and stood up. "I thought we could grab a shower."

He chased her into the bathroom, but stopped outside of the shower to remove his bandages.

When he stepped into the shower, her eyes ran over his chest, over his scars. Two large marks ran along his shoulder, almost making an X. Reaching up, she ran her fingers over the mark.

"This looks much better." She smiled up at him and stepped closer.

***

He wrapped his arms around her, both of them, and didn't even feel the slightest twinge.

"How are you healing so fast?" she asked

162

against his skin.

Suddenly, he froze. Taking a step back, he looked down at his marred skin and saw it for what it really was.

A wound that was almost completely healed. He shook his head and blinked his eyes a few times. "Whoa."

"Ethan?" she said, moving closer to him. "What's wrong?"

"This" he said, running his hand over his shoulder. "I need to see my brother." He jumped out of the shower, leaving her standing there with the glass door open and the water falling over the tile floor.

Wrapping a towel around his hips, he grabbed his cell phone and punched his brother's number.

"What?" Mike answered.

"Get your sorry ass over here," he said, sitting on the edge of the bed. "Now."

Less than ten minutes later, Mike and Xtina walked into the room. Mike was still using his cane, heavily.

"What's going on?" Xtina asked first. They both looked like they'd pulled on the first thing they'd found. Xtina had a heavy hoodie on that looked like it was Mike's.

"This," he said, opening his shirt, showing them his scar.

"Ouch." Mike shook his head. "Looks pretty bad."

"No," Brea said from the hallway. Her eyes locked with his as she walked into the room. "Trust me, it's a lot better than it was two days ago, when I last changed his bandages."

"What?" Mike said, turning towards him.

"Let me see yours," Ethan said, nodding to his leg.

"Like hell." Mike laughed. "This isn't show-n-tell."

"Mike, I need to see. I mean, I'm almost completely back to normal." He pointed to this shoulder to make his point. "I was shot less than two weeks ago. And now, all I have is this scar. Hell, I could probably outlift Jacob at this point. That's not normal."

"Mike," Xtina said, "show him."

Mike's eyes went to Brea.

"Don't be shy. Just drop 'em."

Mike rolled his eyes as Brea turned around.

"Better?" she asked.

Mike sighed then dropped his jeans and showed him his thigh. Slowly he removed his bandages. Ethan noticed there was still dried blood on them.

The nasty scar ran down his upper thigh. It was puckered, red, and looked like it was slowly on the mend.

He walked over and touched the mark, laying a hand solidly over it.

The instant he did, something powerful shot out of his fingertips, causing a strange glow under his hand.

Xtina gasped, and Brea's eyes grew big. Everyone looked on as the light traveled down his fingertips, into his brother's thigh.

Mike jerked several times, then Ethan watched in horror as his brother's eyes rolled to the back of his head as he passed out.

"What the hell!" Ethan said, jerking his hand away. Then he too felt his head spin. Just before he passed out, he saw silver eyes.

Chapter Fifteen

Brea sat across the room in total shock. What she'd just witnessed was even stranger than her teleporting.

"Did he just…heal me?" Mike asked after he woke, looking down at Ethan, who was still unconscious.

Mike's jeans were still around his ankles. Xtina ran her fingers over the fresh scar on Mike's thigh, which, oddly, looked almost identical to the scar on Ethan's shoulder.

"It… It looks like it," Xtina said as Brea shook Ethan, who was waking up.

"What the hell," Ethan said, shaking his head and sitting up straight.

He looked down at his hand in disbelief. Ethan had yet to move. He just sat there, almost in shock.

Before their very eyes, they watched Mike's wound finish completely healing, almost like magic.

"I need a drink," Ethan said, but when he stood up, he fell back to the sofa.

Brea raced over and put her hands on his shoulders, keeping him in place when all his color left him.

"There's some whiskey in the cabinet." Mike pointed to spot over the stove.

Xtina poured a shot in four glasses, then walked over and handed one to each of them.

"Thanks for healing Mike," she said before drinking.

Ethan laughed and then swallowed. He held his glass out, ready for another shot.

"It's ten in the morning," Mike said, shaking his head. He set his glass down, then after another glance at his healed leg, stood and pulled up his jeans.

He walked around, trying out the leg. "It feels good." He did a squat, then another and smiled. "Really good."

"How are you feeling?" Brea asked Ethan.

"Better," he said after the second shot. "Guess I could use some food."

"We're out of pretty much everything. How about we all head into town?" Brea said. "Then, maybe you two would like to head to the lake with us?"

Mike's eyebrows shot up fast. "The lake? The one Jacob and Jess saw last night?"

"Yes, we think it might have something to do with all this."

Brea drove into town with Ethan beside her. He was moving his shoulder and looking down at his hand.

"Are you okay?" she asked as they pulled into the parking lot of the diner.

"Surprisingly, yes." He got out and opened the door for her and then surprised her by pulling her into his arms.

"That was strange," he said, into her hair. "Really strange."

"Yeah, but no stranger than me zapping myself to different places."

"We're not necessarily what most would deem a normal couple." He pulled back and smiled down at her.

"I'm beginning to think that, from now on, nothing is going to be normal again."

Mike and Xtina arrived and they crowded into a booth near the back of the diner. Everyone remained silent until after their food was delivered.

Then Brea leaned forward and glanced at everyone. "Okay, is anyone going to talk about what happened?"

"What is there to talk about?" Xtina said between bites.

Brea shook her head and looked down at her food, not sure she could swallow anything. She leaned forward and lowered her voice. "How about the fact that I can teleport and Ethan can heal people. Not to mention the fact that you can... do what you can."

"I've had a lot longer to cope with these things." Xtina smiled at her. "Besides, we don't know if Ethan can heal just anyone."

"Wait, what do you mean?" Ethan said.

"I mean, it worked on Mike, but who's to say that it will work on just anyone. Besides, gauging from what happened, we know it takes a lot out of you. Both of you." She looked between Mike and Ethan.

"Yeah," Ethan said, taking another bite of his steak. "But this is helping." He smiled.

"Ditto," Mike said, shoveling some meat into his mouth. "But there for a while, I felt like I had the night I got shot."

Ethan nodded. "It was almost..."

"Like I relived that moment," both men said at the same time.

"Whoa, they talk in stereo," Jess said, standing at the edge of the booth. "Care if I join?" she asked, grabbing an empty chair and adding it to the end of the booth before anyone answered.

"So, what are you kids up to today?" She leaned in and grabbed a French fry from Xtina's plate. "Because I was thinking of heading out to the lake."

"We were going to head out there after food," Xtina said. "You're welcome to ride along."

"Yeah," she said, taking some more fries.

"Hey!" Xtina laughed. "You can order some more."

"Yeah, but I like yours better. Besides, I'm not hungry enough for my own."

"Here." Brea nudged her plate towards Jess. "I'm not that hungry. We can share." Jess picked up half of her turkey sandwich and took a bite.

When they left the diner, Jess piled into the back of Xtina's car as Ethan and Brea climbed back into hers.

"What do you think her power is?" Ethan asked, watching them drive away.

"You think she has any?" she asked, pulling out of the parking lot and following Xtina's car.

"Sure, I mean, everyone involved so far has."

"What about Jacob?" she asked.

171

"Jacob?" He groaned. "Hadn't thought about him."

"Why not? I mean, it stands to reason that he'd have something before Jess."

"Why would he? It's not like Mike has…" He turned to her. "Do you know something I don't?"

"No, other than the fact that he's connected to Xtina. And he's been seeing my aunt for over a year," she added as they turned on the highway.

"Yeah, but this." He looked down at his hand. "This is more than just seeing a spirit. This is…"

"Heavy."

He chuckled, then reached over and took her hand. "We'll get through this. I mean, how much weirder could it get?"

They pulled up and parked beside Xtina's car.

"Great," Ethan groaned. "He's here."

Brea glanced over and saw Jacob leaning against the hood of his police car.

"How did he know we were heading here?" he asked as he got out of her car.

"I called him," Jess said, crossing her arms over her chest. "He needs to be here."

"Okay," Ethan said, looking at her. "Why?"

"Because he's part of this." She walked towards him.

Brea noticed the look Jacob gave Jess. It

matched the look that Ethan had given her several times now.

"So," Mike said, walking around the hood of Xtina's car, without so much as a limp, "where do we start?"

***

For some reason, everyone looked to Brea.

"How would I know?" She shrugged and looked at him.

"You've been doing all the research," Jess said. "For the article."

"Article?" Ethan turned towards her. "What would the cult attacking them have to do with your aunt?"

"She's doing an article on me." Xtina smiled, then turned towards Brea. "I've known since the moment you showed up on my porch." She sighed, then wiggled her hand in front of her. "Remember, I have this annoying thing."

Brea sighed. "I may have started out writing about you, but after my first... disappearing act, I changed goals." She leaned against the hood of her car and glanced around at the group. "Since then, I've been researching our parents. All of them."

"Including mine?" Jess asked, something close to fear crossing her eyes.

"Everyone who was there... the night my aunt disappeared."

"How would you know who was there?" Jacob asked.

Brea walked to the back of her car, pulled out her bag, and held out a folder. "Because of this." She pulled out a newspaper article.

Everyone gathered around her and looked at the newspaper article that she'd found.

"It says here that your aunt drowned just off the docks," Jacob said after scanning the article.

"Yes, apparently, there was a party at a lake house near here. She wandered away, and someone saw her fall off the dock. But before they could reach her, she'd sunk below the water and disappeared."

"They never found her body," Jacob added.

"Who claimed they saw her fall in?" Jess asked.

"Your mother," Jacob answered, running a hand over her shoulder.

Ethan noticed the move, but as soon as it happened, Jacob walked away towards the dock a few hundred yards away. Everyone followed him.

They all stood on the dock, looking down at the dark water.

"She's not here." It was Xtina that spoke.

"How do you know?" Jacob asked.

"Trust me, she knows," Mike answered, taking her hand in his.

"If she's not here, then where?" Jacob asked.

"I told you, she's not dead." Xtina looked around at everyone.

"Yeah, you said that before, but what you didn't say was how you know that," Jacob said, tossing a rock into the water.

"It's complicated," she answered. "Why don't we meet back at my place later." Xtina looked over at Jacob. "After you're off shift, so we can go over everything you've learned so far." She turned to Brea.

"I'm done around nine," Jacob said. "I can grab some pizza on my way."

"Can you swing by and pick me up at the diner? I'm filling in for Carla. She's gone into the city for the weekend," Jess said.

"Still don't have your car?" Jacob said.

"Those men call themselves mechanics," she complained as they walked back to the cars. "Thieves is more like it."

"How about I take you back into town," Jacob suggested.

"I want to stick around here for a few minutes more," Ethan said, nodding towards Brea. "If that's okay with you?"

"Sure," she said.

"We have an errand to run." Mike looked at

Xtina. "Then we'll meet you back at the house."

Ethan sat on a park bench with Brea and watched everyone else drive away.

"So?" She turned towards him. "What's the plan?"

He reached over and took her hand, feeling power pulse through the connection.

"Do you feel that?" he asked her.

She looked down at their joined hands. "That's new."

"It feels like something has woken in me," he said, feeling the pulse radiating between them.

"What do we do now?" she asked him, leaning her head against his shoulder. He smiled when he realized that all his pain was gone.

Chapter Sixteen

They made their way back to the local grocery store. She'd never gone grocery shopping with a man before. With all her boyfriends, she'd never shared this simple domestic task.

She was basically living with Ethan now. And she liked shopping with him. Turns out that they liked the same foods. He made her laugh, which was something no other man had ever done. Most of her other relationships had been so serious. There had been passion, but not laughter.

By the time they drove back to the house, she had pretty much forgotten about their odd experiences. But then she stepped up to the porch and instead of walking into Mike's house, walked into a dark, damp, smelly room.

This time, instead of just feeling her skin tingling, her head throbbed, and her shoulders, neck, and back ached like she'd slept on them wrong. Her lungs burned as if she were sitting around a fire.

She blinked a few times to get her bearings. It was dark and it took almost a minute for her eyes to adjust.

She took one step forward and then another and entered a large room. There were nine people in the room with her, laughing, drinking, and listening to music. She noticed that the full moon was high over the opening of the circular room.

No one seemed to notice her, so she walked into the room fully.

She noticed her father first. His younger self. Her eyes moved to the woman he was kissing and her heart sank. It was her aunt Misty, not her mother. Looking around, she found her mother sitting in the corner, writing in a small journal. The journal she'd discovered on her sixteenth birthday. The one that had inspired her to become a journalist.

She saw her mother glance up and sigh when she noticed the couple kissing.

Turning her eyes away, she took in as much as she could about the other three couples. Xtina's parents were sitting along the wall, heavily making out. Jacob, Mike, and Ethan's parents were in the corner talking quietly. From the looks of it, she was already pregnant with Jacob, but hiding it.

Their mother kept putting her hands on her flat stomach, with a sad and worried look in her eyes.

Then she turned to Jess's parents and moved closer to them.

They were talking, laughing, and drinking beer.

"Hey," Jess's mother said suddenly. "I've got an idea."

Everyone in the room zoned in on her, then moved closer around the circle of water.

"How about we have some real fun?"

Suddenly, Brea was zipped back to the front porch. Ethan's hands moved to her shoulders and pulled her in tight.

"You're back," he said, running his hands over her arms, rubbing warmth into them. "You're freezing." He pulled her into the house.

There was a fire burning in the fireplace and Xtina and Mike stood just inside.

"Is she okay?" Xtina asked.

"Yes, just cold," Ethan said, moving her closer to the fireplace.

Mike handed them a blanket, which Ethan wrapped around her.

"Here, drink this." Xtina handed her a beer.

Brea took a drink and instantly felt better. She sat down on the sofa, reaching out to the warmth of the fire.

"How long was I gone?" she asked when she

felt a little steadier.

"Half an hour," Ethan answered, looking worried. "We really need to focus on learning how to control this whole... thing." He pulled her closer. "And the sooner the better."

"I'm sorry," she said, reaching out and touching his hand. She'd never thought of how her leaving made him feel each time.

"Where'd you go?" Ethan finally asked.

"I guess I was in the silo. The night my aunt disappeared." She shivered remembering what had happened.

"Can you tell us what you saw?" Xtina said.

"You time traveled?" Ethan asked, interrupting.

"Yeah, I guess so. I mean, everyone was there. All of our parents and my aunt." She pulled her hair away from her face.

"And?" Mike asked.

"Why don't we wait until the others show up," Xtina said. "That way she can get some rest." Xtina stood up and took Mike's hand. "Let's head back to the house, give them some time before everyone else shows up. We'll see you in a few hours."

"You okay?" Ethan asked once they were alone. His hands went into her hair as he pulled her close.

She didn't get a chance to answer, before his

180

lips were on hers.

"You scared me," he said between kisses.

"I'm sorry," she said again, pulling back slowly.

"You broke the eggs."

"What?"

"When you did your whole vanishing act, you had the grocery sack with the eggs in it." He chuckled.

She laughed. "So, I don't take everything I'm holding with me then."

"It would appear not." He kissed her again. "Do you want to tell me what happened?"

"They were hanging out. Partying. My mother…" A tear slipped from her eyes. "They were so young." He reached up, wiped the tear with his fingertip. "My father and aunt were together. My mother sat in the corner, her nose buried in a book. My father always said that he'd never really noticed her until Misty was gone." She shook her head.

"What else did you notice?" he asked.

"Your parents were there. Your mother must have already been pregnant with Jacob."

She felt him tense, his eyes turning towards her.

"What happened next?" His voice shook.

"Jess's mother stepped forward. She asked if

everyone wanted to have some fun."

"And?"

"And, then I came back."

***

Several hours later, Ethan sat in Xtina's living room, listening to Brea retell her story. Everyone in the room was on the edge of their seats.

When she was done talking, everyone turned their eyes to Jess.

"Where are your parents?" Mike asked.

"Gone," Jess said, walking over to the fire.

"Any clue?" he asked.

"None." She turned to the room. "Listen, I'd love to be of some help, but if I knew where they were hiding, I would have kicked their asses long ago." She crossed her arms over her chest.

"Right," Xtina said. "So, let's lay out the facts, shall we?"

She pulled out a large folder and set it on the coffee table. "Did you bring everything?" she asked Brea and Jess.

"Yes," both said in unison. Jess pulled out a thick book, while Brea took out her tablet and flipped it open.

Another hour later, they stopped working to eat the Chinese food that had been delivered.

"Okay, is anyone else's head hurting?" Ethan

asked his brothers when the ladies went into the kitchen to get fresh drinks. He glanced down at the charts and calendars they had made.

"I know they think that all of this"—he motioned to the scattered papers around the coffee table— "is supposed to make things clearer, but I'm just not seeing it."

"Neither am I," Mike said. "And this is what I do for a living." Mike ran a hand through his hair.

"Listen, I know they want to find answers, but I think it's all just a big waste of our time," Jacob added quietly.

They all turned when the women came back into the room.

"We've been talking," Xtina said, glancing around the room.

Jess walked into the room holding a tray of six crystal glasses.

"What is this going to accomplish?" Jacob asked as Jess set the tray down on top of all the papers on the coffee table.

"At least it's something," Jess said.

Everyone was quiet for a moment. Then one by one, they sat down around the coffee table.

"May the best of our past be the worst of our future," Jess said, holding up her glass.

"Do you have a whole library of those in your

head?" Jacob asked, before holding up his own glass.

Jess smiled and shrugged.

"To answers," Xtina said, sealing the toast with a clink.

Just like before, the light blinded them.

And like before, he stood in the field with the waxing moon overhead. Unlike last time, he made a point to notice everything. Every detail.

The night was oddly warm, considering the last few weeks had been chilly.

Brea was wearing a large hoodie, jeans, and boots. Her hair was tied back in a long braid.

He was walking towards her, and like before, he watched her disappear. Slowly. She screamed no, like before.

But this time was different. After she'd gone, instead of returning, he stuck around the field longer. Suddenly time sped up and he saw himself, night after night, returning to the same spot, until the full moon hung low in the sky over the field.

He saw a flash and heard Brea's scream as her image blinked in and out in front of him. Something caught his eye and he looked skyward, and what he saw made his skin crawl. It appeared as if a comet was falling from the sky. He looked again and realized it wasn't a comet. It was the moon.

Seconds later, he was back in Xtina's living room, along with everyone else.

Chapter Seventeen

Brea leaned back on the sofa and felt the blood drain from her face. Everyone else in the room was silent as they looked around at each other.

"What was that?" Mike asked. "What did I just see?"

Jess stood up and walked to the window and glanced out. "That was the end of the world."

"My god!" Jacob stood up and walked over to lay a hand on Jess's shoulders.

"How do we stop it?" Xtina said, reaching over and taking Mike's hand. "What can we do?"

Everyone looked around at each other.

"There has to be a way," she said when no one spoke. "Why would we be seeing all this? What other reason than to stop it." Her voice had risen slightly.

"The moon is going to fall in less than a month," Jacob said, putting his arm around Jess, who turned and started sobbing into his shoulder.

"There has to be a way to stop it," Xtina repeated. She set the tray aside and started going through the papers again. "It's got to be here."

"Xtina." Mike took her hand, stopping her. "We'll find a way."

"There is." Brea stood up slowly. "Only one way," she said, moving to the fire. Her entire body was freezing, right down to her soul.

"How? What did you see?" Ethan asked, moving over to her.

"Everything," she whispered. "Everything that's supposed to happen. Everything that shouldn't."

"And?" Jess asked.

"And, I have to learn how to control this…power." She looked down at her hands and closed her eyes, remembering the pain and suffering she'd seen. The pain and suffering she'd caused because she'd screwed up.

She couldn't stop her tears from sliding down her face.

By the time they walked back across the field towards the house, she was exhausted. Every ounce of her body ached, like she'd run a marathon and then another one.

"Are you okay?" Ethan asked as he shut the door behind them.

"Yeah, I just need some rest." She toed off her shoes, then peeled off her jacket.

"How about a hot bath instead?" He walked over to her and wrapped his arms around her.

"That actually sounds amazing." She rested her head against his chest. She took a moment to listen to his heartbeat against her cheek.

"Why don't you head in there. I've got a call to make." When she looked at him in question, he sighed. "My folks. I think it's about time I got some answers."

Since her head was throbbing, the idea of escaping into the bathroom for an hour by herself sounded amazing.

Taking a step back, she took his hands. "Go easy on them."

His chuckle stopped her. "From what we just saw, we have less than a month before the end of the world and my folks may or may not know something about it." He ran his hands through his hair and walked to the fireplace, putting both hands on the mantel.

"I meant about your brother."

He turned to her. "That's the last thing on my mind."

Brea walked over and kissed him.

"I'll be in in a while." He turned away and pulled out his phone.

She walked into the bathroom and shut the door behind her. When she leaned against it, she closed her eyes as images of what she'd seen flashed behind them.

She started running a bath and peeled off her clothes. When she stepped into the water, she sighed at how wonderful it felt to have the warmth spread through her.

Her muscles relaxed slowly, releasing the pain in her head and shoulders. Dipping her head under the water, she tried to keep her mind off what she'd seen.

So many question ran through her mind. Should she tell Ethan and the others what she'd seen after she'd disappeared in the field?

Something told her she had to keep it quiet. At least until she could work out some of the details for herself.

She sat up from the water and rested back. There were too many things to think about. Did she really believe she could control her powers?

She looked at her hands, her arms, her entire body. In the past few weeks, she'd tried everything, silently willing her body to move through space and time to another location.

Nothing had worked. What had she done before? What had she been thinking or feeling each time she'd vanished?

Her mind raced over every time she'd vanished from one place and appeared another, trying to tie something together. Find some pattern.

By the time she climbed out of the lukewarm water, her headache was completely gone. Her body, thankfully, was gloriously loose.

Wrapping a towel around her, she wiped the fog from the mirror so she could stare at her reflection.

She'd lost weight, which caused her hips to stick out farther than before. Great, just what she needed.

She reached for a brush but stopped when she saw the figure move behind her.

"How did it go with your folks?" She turned around, only to feel every ounce of warmth she'd just gained from the bath leave her.

Her first thought was that her aunt Misty had changed. She took a step back, and a scream caught in her throat.

The woman floated towards her.

Her gray eyes bore into Brea's silver ones.

"Leave what's been done alone," she said, moving closer until Brea backed up against the sink.

"Who are you?" she asked when she'd found her voice. But as soon as she asked, she knew.

"Leave the past alone," she said, taking a step back and fading in front of Brea's eyes.

"The world is going to die," Brea said, causing the woman to stop and look at her.

"Fate has been written," she said before disappearing. When Brea was alone, she heard one final whisper. "You can't stop it."

***

Ethan punched in his parents' number the second Brea went into the bathroom.

His mother answered on the second ring. "Hi, Ethan. How are you feeling?"

"Much better," he said, running his hand over his forehead. "Mom, I need you to get dad on speakerphone."

"Has something happened?" His mother's voice turned concerned instantly.

"Just get him." He moved over to the cabinet that held his brother's hard liquor.

By the time his dad got on the phone, he had swallowed two fingers of some very good bourbon. He made a mental note to remember the brand name.

"What's up son?" His father's voice stopped him from taking another sip.

"I need you both to be completely honest with me for the next few minutes." He swallowed the drink. "Can you do that?"

192

There was silence, then his mother asked. "What's this all about?"

"Mom, just answer yes or no."

"Yes, of course."

"Dad?"

"Son, I'd like to know what—"

"Dad, just give me a few minutes. I'll tell you what this is all about soon."

He heard his dad sigh and then clear his throat.

"Sure, fine."

"What happened the winter before your senior year?"

"What do you mean?"

"The winter you found out you were pregnant with Jacob."

Once again, the phone was silent. He waited, knowing his mother would talk soon enough.

"How do you know about Jacob?" his mother finally said.

"Susan," his father said, stopping her. He heard the phone switch off from speaker. "Listen Ethan, things were different back then."

"Dad, I don't care about what you did about Jacob. I'm talking about what happened the night you all threw a party in the silo."

He heard his father hold his breath then release

193

it.

"The night Misty disappeared," he added, growing more frustrated.

"Misty drowned," his father added.

"Don't pull that bullshit with me."

"You watch your language, son." The tone in his father's voice made him take a deep breath to calm himself down.

"If you'd just seen what I did, you'd be pissed too. Tell me what you guys did."

"We didn't do anything," he added.

"You must have done something. What?" He growled it out.

"Rusty, let me talk," his mother said.

"Honey, talk to Rachelle. She knows everything. We just wanted to have one last party before…"

"Rachelle?" he asked.

"Baker. Rachelle Baker and Larry Sorenson."

"Jess's parents? Why ask her? Don't you know what happened?"

They were quiet for a moment, then his father said, "Not exactly. We were—"

"We don't really remember," his mother broke in. "Rachelle's the only one who didn't… black out."

He sighed and closed his eyes.

"We lost track of everyone from back then," his father added. "After…"

"Do you have any clue where they are? We've looked," Ethan added, figuring he wasn't going to get any further with his parents.

"No, like your father said, we haven't talked to anyone from Hidden Creek in years."

He hung up the phone more frustrated than before.

He tossed his phone on the counter and made his way to the bathroom to check in on Brea.

When he walked into the bathroom, she was standing at the sink, wrapped in a towel, crying.

He gathered her into his arms and held her until she stopped crying.

"We can't stop it," she cried into his chest. "I've seen it. There's nothing we can do to change what happens."

"We'll figure it out," he said, but deep in his heart, the darkness was almost too much to bear. "Somehow, we'll figure it out." He pulled back, taking her face in his hands, until their eyes met. "Together. All of us."

"What if we don't?" she asked, and he wiped a tear from her cheek.

"We will." He leaned down and placed a kiss on

her lips. "We will."

Chapter Eighteen

The next morning, Brea felt a little steadier. She'd gotten a few hours of sleep, with the help of Ethan. He'd held onto her all night and just hearing his steady breathing helped calm her.

He even made them blueberry pancakes and scrambled eggs with bacon. She felt almost human after dressing for the day.

She wasn't surprised when she walked out of the bedroom and found Mike and Xtina in the living room with Rose at their feet.

"Ethan asked us to come over to talk about his conversation with our folks," Mike said, wrapping an arm around Xtina's shoulders.

Ethan waited until Brea sat down in the chair closest to the fireplace. Ever since last night in the bathroom, she was finding it hard to get warm.

"What have you found out about Jess's

198

parents?" Ethan turned to Mike.

"Not much. After doing some research, I still haven't been able to track them down. It's like the second Jess turned thirteen, they pulled a vanishing act." Mike shook his head.

"What do you remember about them?" Ethan asked Xtina.

"Not much. I was too busy trying to grow up and not stand out too much. From what I do remember, they were never very protective of Jess. They pretty much let her run around on her own. Then, poof, they disappeared."

"What did the town have to say?" Ethan asked.

"What do you mean?" Xtina asked.

"Well, from what I've learned, the people in this town do a lot of chatting. I can't see a couple leaving their teen alone without the town saying something."

"Sure, there was talk." She glanced around. "Some rumors had them moving to Tahiti, others said they were running from the law."

"The law?" Mike asked.

"Yeah, they used to own the coffee shop. Actually, Jess's parents used to own half the town."

"What exactly happened?" Ethan asked.

"Well, no one really knows anything except that

they high-tailed it out of town with all their money, leaving their thirteen-year-old with nothing but a beat-up truck and a suitcase full of clothes."

There was a lot of anger in Xtina's voice when she talked about what Jess had been through.

"Why would they leave?" Mike asked. "Don't get me wrong—from the sounds of it, they wouldn't have won any parent of the year awards. But hightailing it out of town so quickly?" He shook his head. "That doesn't sound right."

"So, there was something else," Brea said. "Something darker that took them away."

"What are you thinking?" Ethan asked.

"From what I saw the other night, Rachelle, Jess's mother, was in charge of the weird stuff."

"What do you mean?" Ethan turned to her.

"Well, she's the one that stopped the party and asked if everyone wanted to have some real fun." She looked at Ethan. "And…she appeared to me last night."

"What?" everyone said at the same time, including Ethan. He reached over and took her hands.

"Why didn't you tell me?" he said after a moment.

"I needed some time to process." She sighed. "I'm sorry, I was scared."

"What happened?" Xtina asked.

"She told me—warned me—not to look into the past."

"Does that mean that Jess's mother is dead?"

"No." Brea shook her head. "She appeared to me, like... teleported." She looked around at everyone. "But she could control it."

"How do you know?" Mike asked.

She felt a shiver down her spine. "I just do."

"Why would she warn us? Did she say anything else?" Xtina asked.

"She told me to leave the past alone. That fate has been written and that we can't stop it." A shiver ran down her body.

"What does that even mean?" Mike asked.

"This makes one thing clear," Ethan added. "We need to find her. And we need to do it now." Brea leaned forward and grabbed her laptop and got to work.

She glanced up to find everyone just watching her.

"Well? Don't you each have some way you could help?" she asked.

Mike jumped up and pulled Xtina up with him. "Yeah, we can..."

"I could talk to Carla," Xtina said.

"Carla?" Brea stopped her typing and waited.

"Jess's godmother. She kind of took the mama bear position after the Sorensons left."

"Good," Brea said.

"I've got some other ways to look for the Sorensons," Mike added. "Maybe you can help me out, Ethan?"

"Sure." Ethan got up. "Will you be okay here?"

"Yeah." She glanced back down at her laptop.

She heard them all leave and decided to make a few calls.

When the doorbell rang a while later, she stood up and stretched. Glancing down at her watch, she realized she'd been at it for almost two hours.

Shaking her arms and fingers out, she opened the front door.

Drew stood on the porch, leaning against the door jam.

"I thought you went home." She leaned against the door.

"You thought wrong." He chuckled. "I've gone over everything you sent me," he said, skirting her and walking into the living room.

She tried to stop him, but he ducked around her and made his way to the fireplace.

"Working on something?" His eyes had zeroed in on her screen, so she walked over and shut her laptop, then crossed her arms over her chest.

"I gave you everything—"

"Come on, Brea. We both know that's bull. You gave me tidbits. I had to ask myself why you'd hold back." He sat down on the leather chair. "So, I'm going to sit here until I get to the bottom of this conundrum"

"Drew, there's nothing. Xtina is clean. Besides, I've heard from the local police that Laura Schmitt's case is cracking fast now that they've pulled her phone records."

She moved over to the table and watched him, knowing he could wait patiently until he got what he wanted. Annoyingly so.

"So?" He chuckled. "I'm not here about some housewife and a murder for hire."

"Then what?" She waited.

"You know why I'm here."

"I'm not coming back—" she started, but his laughter stopped him.

"There will come a time when you'll come begging. But for now, I'll settle for the whole story." He nodded to her laptop.

Her eyes narrowed as he walked over to her. When he reached out and flicked a finger over her shoulder, she jerked away.

"There's only so much I can handle," she warned. "Why don't you back off?"

His smile grew, but he took a step back. "As you wish."

She hated it that he could pour on the charm when he tried. "Why are you really here? What's in Hidden Creek that you want so bad?"

"We've been over this." He tucked his hands in his jean pockets.

"Me? Really?" She chuckled. "I'm pretty sure I've made myself clear on this. If it's the story, I've given you what I have." Just talking to Drew was making her head spin. He was playing her; she was sure of it. Confusing her.

"Brea." His tone told her that her lies weren't going to cover it anymore.

She sighed and tilted her head. "Fine, I have some... information I've kept."

"Like?" he asked.

"I'll send you the files."

He laughed. "Oh no. We've played this game before. I wait two days to get a bunch of stuff I could have found on my own with a few key strokes."

She waited. "So? Where does that leave us?"

"Well, from where I'm standing, it leaves us right here"—he pulled out a chair and sat down—"until I have everything I want."

She laughed. "Right, well, have fun." She walked towards the door, ready to leave him sitting alone in Mike's house.

"I have some information you want," he said.

"Right," she said without turning around. "What could you possibly have that I want?"

Her hand was on the doorknob.

"The whereabouts of your father," he said, stopping her hand.

"He's traveling," she said, feeling her stomach roll. She'd been trying to call him, but all she'd gotten was his voicemail.

"Right," Drew said. "A US congressmen goes traveling for weeks without telling his secretary or daughter where."

She turned towards him. "He does that all the time."

His chuckle stopped her and made her gut sink. It was a lie. Every time he'd traveled for work, Jane, his secretary, had always known where. But when she'd called the woman a few days ago, Jane didn't know where he was. Actually, she'd sounded very worried herself.

"What do you know?" She moved towards him.

He stood up slowly, and his eyes moved to her computer. "You give me what I want, I'll share what I have."

****

Ethan was growing more frustrated by the

moment. Mike was good at his job, really good, but after a few hours of dead ends, he was beginning to think that finding Jess's parents was impossible.

Wherever they were, they were doing everything they could to make sure no one found them. The big question was why.

Why would a seemingly normal couple from one of America's perfect small towns go into such deep hiding that no one could find anything about them in over ten years.

The day the Sorensons left Hidden Creek, they might as well have hopped on a rocket and left the earth.

The short walk back to the house helped clear his frustration a little. The cool air helped him see things straight.

When he climbed the back stairs, he stopped cold when he saw a man standing in his brother's living room, holding Brea by the shoulders.

He took a deep breath and stepped in the back door, smiling slightly when Drew stepped away from Brea and dropped his hands.

Brea looked relieved to see him.

"Looks like I'm missing the party." He walked over to stand next to Brea.

Drew sat down at the table and smiled. "More like a business meeting."

"Really?" he said, glancing at Brea.

"Drew was just leaving." Brea crossed her arms over her chest.

"Not until after we have a chat about Congressmen Garrett."

Ethan turned towards Brea. "Your father is a congressman?"

Brea nodded slightly, then turned back to Drew.

"Like I said, my father is just traveling."

Ethan saw her fidget with her cell phone in her pocket and he knew she was worried. He'd heard her leaving a message for him yesterday.

"What do you know about him?" Ethan moved closer.

Drew chuckled. "Well, I was just about to tell Brea, but she has something I want first."

"What?" She sat down, tucking her hands in her lap, something she did when she was lying. "What could I possibly have?"

"We all know you kept information from me," Drew said. "What I don't understand is why you're having such a problem doing your job?"

"I don't have a job," she countered.

Drew tilted his head.

"Is that what all this is about?" He tapped his fingers on the table. "You're waiting for an offer?"

Drew's eyes roamed over Brea, causing Ethan's blood to boil. He stepped between them.

"I no longer care about working at WSB," Brea said in a strong voice.

"How about anywhere in Atlanta?" Drew's eyes narrowed.

"Are you threatening her?" Ethan stepped forward.

"No, just letting her know how deep my influence runs." Drew stood up. "You promised me a story." He looked at Brea. "Either you deliver or your reputation will be ruined."

He walked towards the door, but stopped before leaving. "If I were you, I'd ask why your father made a trip to The Rock before pulling his vanishing act."

The moment Drew left, Brea relaxed. "I'm sorry." She closed her eyes and rested her head in her hands.

He took her into his arms, holding her tight. "Why didn't you tell me about your dad?"

She sighed. "I get radio silence from him all the time."

"But?" He pulled back and looked into her silver eyes.

"But, this time it's different."

"How?"

"The last time I talked to him, something was off. I mentioned Hidden Creek and suddenly he had to go. I haven't heard from him since."

"We'll figure this out," he said into her hair. He pulled back and lifted her face to his. When he placed a kiss on her lips, a sudden urgency filled him. "Brea?"

She shook her head. "No, just hold me."

He wrapped his arms around her tighter.

"What didn't you give him?"

She sighed into his chest. "More information."

"On?"

"Everyone. He doesn't need to know everything." She sighed.

He pulled back and looked at her, then lifted her up and carried her back to the bedroom. When he laid her down on the bed, she sighed and pulled him down with her.

He couldn't describe how he felt when their lips met. What touching her did to him.

He took his time peeling her clothes from her body. When he touched her, his hands shook and he had to pull away so he could have a moment.

Brea didn't give him a chance. Her legs wrapped around his hips and pulled him closer to her. It was like she hypnotized him. Controlled him. He moved without thought and slowly slid into her heat, taking her slowly until he felt everything that had been building inside of him over the past few months' finally release.

Chapter Nineteen

*B*rea couldn't stop her body from melting against Ethan's. She'd never felt anything like this before.

Her mind shot to an image of her standing in the field, finally admitting to herself and to him that she was in love.

She sat up and reached for her shirt.

"Are you okay?" Ethan asked, rolling aside.

"Yes," she lied, keeping her back to him. "I wanted to do some more research."

"I'll help."

"No," she said quickly, glancing back at him. She needed some time to think and according to their chart and calendar, they had less than a week before she was supposed to pull her vanishing act. "Why don't you order us some food?"

She grabbed her clothes and walked to the bathroom, then leaned against the door until her heart settled. What was she doing? Was she falling into the trap of believing in fate?

A shiver ran through her when she remembered Xtina's words in the store. "Hidden Creek holds your fate."

She splashed cold water on her face, then looked at her reflection.

"Fate has been written," Jess's mother had said before disappearing. "You can't stop it." The woman's whisper echoed in her mind.

"No," she said to the empty room. "I refuse to believe I'm destined to fade away forever. Lost." She straightened her shoulders and pulled on her clothes, then brushed her hair and walked out of the bathroom feeling more clearheaded.

She found Ethan in the kitchen, cooking. Without saying a word, she sat in front of her computer and started searching.

When Ethan sat a plate of grilled cheese in front of her, she ate it without glancing away from the screen.

"Drew said The Rock." She finally glanced up. Ethan sat across from her on his own laptop.

"Yeah. He said, 'Find out why your father made a trip to the rock before pulling his vanishing act.'"

"I was thinking it was some sort of... bar or

something, but it's a town." She glanced up at him across from the table. "And it's only an hour away."

He stood up. "I'll drive."

"Wait." She stopped him. "I'm not sure this is the place." She shook her head. "I can't find any mention of the town in my father's records."

"Your father's records?" he asked, moving closer to her.

"His emails and his journals."

"You have access to all that?"

"I might have guessed his password." She shrugged. "He's my father," she said when Ethan just looked at her.

"Sure, and a US congressmen. Isn't that against several federal laws?"

"Not if I guessed his passwords. He did rent a car the day after I spoke to him last." She leaned back. "He hasn't returned it."

"Was it an in-state rental?" he asked.

She pulled up the email with the receipt and scanned it. "Yes." Her eyes met his.

"Then I'd say an hour drive is worth it." He stood up. "I'll drive," he repeated.

The entire trip to The Rock, they talked about her father. How he'd grown up, how he'd raised her by himself. Ethan asked if he'd been acting weird before the phone call. She couldn't remember anything. Not until she'd mentioned she was in Hidden Creek.

"Do you really think he's here somewhere?" Ethan asked, when they pulled into the small town. There was one flashing red light in the town and they pulled into the only gas station just off the highway.

"You have the make and model of the car?" Ethan asked.

"Yes." She gave it to him.

"I'll be right back." He got out of the car and went inside the small gas station store.

She worried for the first time that something might have happened to her father. She checked her phone for what seemed like the millionth time that day for messages.

Once more, she punched her dad's number, only to get sent to his voicemail.

"Dad? Give me a call as soon as you get this message. I'm really worried about you." She hung up and closed her eyes.

The car door opened and she glanced over at Ethan.

"Well?" she asked before he got a chance to fully get in.

"The clerk remembers seeing your father last week. He says he came in and asked for

215

directions."

"To?" Her heart skipped.

"A ranch just outside of town." He turned on the car and glanced over at her. "It's about ten minutes outside of town."

"A ranch?"

He nodded. "On Rocky Bottom Road." He pulled out of the gas station.

"What did he say about my father? Did he look well?"

Ethan nodded. "The clerk says he thought your father looked agitated. Like he was in a hurry." Ethan shook his head. "But then the clerk probably thought that about me too."

She took a deep breath. "Okay, so now what? We go to the ranch?"

"That's my thinking." He turned off the main highway.

"Then what? What if he's not there?" She bit her bottom lip.

"Then we find out where he went." He reached over and took her hand in his. "We'll find him."

"Yeah, but when we do, what comes next? It's not like he has the answers on how to stop the end of the world."

Ethan sighed. "No, but he may know something more about it. Something that could help us solve the mystery." He dropped her hand and turned the car one more time onto a dirt road.

Finally, they stopped in front of a large sign that said Rock Bottom Ranch.

"Look," Ethan said, nodding towards the end of the driveway. There, parked in front of a two-story home that looked like it had been built over a century ago, sat her father's rental car.

Ethan parked her car next to it. She jumped out of the car before it had stopped.

By the time she'd knocked on the front door, Ethan was standing beside her.

She heard several people moving around inside, including a dog or two.

When the door opened, she was holding her breath and wasn't prepared for what she saw looking back at her. Standing there, in a "Kiss the Cook" apron, stood a woman she'd believed to be dead. A woman with silver blue eyes and a smile that matched her own.

"Mom?" Brea said just before blacking out.

***

"What in the hell?" Ethan said, snatching up Brea before she hit the wood planks of the porch. His eyes narrowed as he looked at the woman standing just inside the door.

Shifting Brea into his arms, he barged into the house and looked around. Seeing three other people sitting around a kitchen table, he glared at Brea's father as he set Brea gently down on the sofa.

When she was safely cushioned, he turned on the four people.

"What in the hell have you done?"

"Who are you?" Jess's father stood up slowly.

"Easy." Brea's father stood up and rushed over to kneel beside her. His hands shook as he reached up and touched his daughter's face. "Brea?" He slapped it slightly, causing her to stir.

"Who are you?" This time it was Rachelle Sorenson who asked.

"I'm Ethan Kincaid." He turned to them. "You're Jess's parents." It wasn't a question.

"Yes," Rachelle said after a moment.

He turned to Brea's mother. "You're Dawn? Brea's mother?" His eyes narrowed, then turned to Jess's father.

The woman refused to meet his eyes. Instead, her eyes were glued to Brea and he saw tears sliding down her cheeks.

Instead of answering him, she asked Byron. "Is she okay?"

"It's a little late for you to show your motherly concern, isn't it?" He stood between her and Brea and then turned to her father. "You told her all these years that her mother was dead."

218

Byron shook Brea lightly, and when her eyes fluttered open, Ethan walked over and pushed him aside.

"You okay?" he asked, concern flooding his voice.

Brea's eyes blinked a few times as she looked around the room. Her gaze landed on her mother.

"Mom?" Brea sat up, but he stopped her from getting up.

"Easy." He sat next to her. "Take a moment." He took her hand.

Anger and hurt appeared behind her eyes. "You lied." Her eyes landed on her father. "All these years." Her voice was low.

"Brea—" her father started to say.

"No!" she screamed and stood up, walking over to her father and stopping less than a foot away. "You lied! Why?"

"Your mother…" Byron's eyes moved to Dawn. "She was sick."

"Sick! Not dead." Brea crossed her arms over her chest and took a step back. Then she turned to Dawn. Her eyes ran up and down the woman. "Sick, not dead," she repeated softly.

"Honey." Dawn held out her hands and moved closer.

"No!" Brea jerked away. "You don't get to

speak to me like you know me. Just because you gave birth to me, doesn't mean you know me."

"You're right," Dawn said, her eyes turning down.

"We'll leave…" Jess's mother said, reaching for her husband's hand.

"No one is leaving," Ethan said, looking around the room. "Not until we have some answers."

"Why?" Brea turned to her father. "Why did you hide this?"

"Dawn wasn't the same after Misty's… accident."

Brea's eyes narrowed. "The truth," she said. "No more lies."

Her father took a deep breath and glanced around at the other people in the room. "Very well, let's all sit down." He nodded towards the sofa and chairs.

Ethan noticed that Byron had taken the spot directly next to Dawn. When they were all settled, Byron started.

He reached over and took the woman's hand in his. "Dawn wasn't the same after her sister disappeared. We tried to get on with our lives, but shortly after you were born, something just…"—his eyes met Dawn's—"clicked inside her. She began to act out of sorts." He glanced over at the other couple. "We were concerned that she would hurt you."

"Hurt me?" Brea asked. "Why?"

"I found her putting baking soda in your bottle," Rachelle said, a tear sliding down her face. Her husband reached over and wrapped his arm around her. "I started staying with her, during the day while your father was at work, you know, to watch out for her and you. But then, I found her pouring boiling water into the bathtub one day. She was preparing you for bath time like there wasn't anything wrong with sticking a two-week-old baby in one-hundred-degree water."

"That's when we knew there was something wrong," Byron added. "We checked her into the best clinic."

"Why the ruse of her death?" Brea asked.

"I was running for state representative at the time."

Brea stood up and walked to the front window and looked out. "Let me guess, you didn't think having a wife locked up would look good on the resume?"

Byron glanced over at him. "We thought it was for the best."

"Why is she here, now?" Brea turned and nodded towards her mother.

"Last week," Byron said, "the day that you called, I got a message from Rach and Larry. The home had called and told them that Dawn had woken up."

"Woken?" Brea asked.

"I don't know how it's possible, but the day you showed up in Hidden Creek, I snapped out of whatever it was that had been holding me." Dawn leaned forward, her eyes searching Brea's. "It was like a dream. Everything. I don't even remember giving birth to you." A tear escaped her silver eyes. "You have to believe me. I would have never hurt you."

Brea shook her head and took a step towards the door. "I…" She turned and walked out of the house.

Ethan started to get up.

"No, let me." Her father put a hand on his shoulder, then followed Brea.

Ethan glanced around at the other people. "Okay, so that explains why she did a vanishing act." He nodded to Dawn. "What's your excuse for leaving a thirteen-year-old girl to fend for herself?"

Chapter Twenty

$\mathcal{B}$rea ran away from the house until she was out of breath. Her sides hurt, but not as bad as her heart did. Closing her eyes, she rested against a tree and took several deep breaths until she felt the chill of the day hit her.

Here, where the pine and oak trees were thick, the air was a lot cooler. Turning around, she sat with her back against the tree and cried.

When she heard a branch snap close to her, she jerked her head up as her father moved towards her.

"Hey, pumpkin." He sat down next to her, his

back to the same tree. "Are you okay?"

She laughed. "Am I okay? I just found out that my father, the man whom I always believed would never lie to me, has lied to me my entire life. Oh, and my dead mother wasn't really dead." She dusted her hands on her jeans, then crossed her arms over her knees.

"I know it's a lot to take in." He reached over and set his hand over hers. "I'm sorry. I thought I had done the right thing."

Hearing his voice crack, she glanced over at him.

"How could I tell my little girl that her mother was crazy? What would that have done to you?" He shook his head and she watched in horror as a tear escaped his blue eyes. She could only remember seeing her father cry one time before. The day she'd moved out on her own.

"Dad?" She took his hand in his. "I would have dealt with it."

He shook his head. "But I couldn't." He closed his eyes. "I loved your mother, but after all these years, I had to owe up to the fact that I wasn't in love with her. Not when we married."

"Misty?" she asked, already knowing the answer. "You loved Misty."

Her father's eyes met hers. "Yes, but when she disappeared…"

"Disappeared, not died." Brea's eyes narrowed.

"Honey, there's so much we need to talk about." He glanced around, then stood up and held out his hands. "It's getting dark and cold. Let's go back to the house and have some dinner. Your mother has made spaghetti." He sighed. "She always loved to cook."

She allowed her father to help her up, but stiffened when he pulled her into a hug. "I'm sorry," he said into her hair. "I'm so sorry for lying to you. I should have told you... when you were old enough to understand."

She sighed and pulled away. "You shouldn't have lied." She walked back to the house with her father following close behind.

When they entered the house, Ethan was standing over Jess's father.

"Is everything okay?" Brea walked over and laid a hand on Ethan's shoulder.

"This... These people..." Ethan ran his hands through his hair and stepped back. "They left a thirteen-year-old to fend for herself because they were afraid of her."

Jess's mother was crying, bawling into her husband's shoulders.

"You." Brea stood next to Ethan. "You appeared to me."

Rachelle looked up at her. Her tears dried up quickly as her eyes narrowed.

"I don't know what you're talking about." The woman's entire demeanor changed. Her shoulders straightened and her eyes cleared.

"You showed up in my bathroom." She almost screamed it. "Threatened me. Told me to not look into the past. Why?"

Ethan walked around the room. She could tell he was frustrated. "They own Jess an explanation."

"Yes, and we will see that she gets one," Brea said. "But now, I want to know why that woman showed up in my bathroom and threatened me. Told me to leave the past alone."

"You've seen it," Rachelle said. "You've seen what happens when you meddle."

"What?" Brea shook her head.

"The moon?" Ethan added. "That happens because of us?"

"Why else?" Rachelle said, her eyes narrowing. "We had set everything right, but then... you showed up." She turned to Ethan. "And everything changed."

"How do you know about it?" Brea asked.

Jess's father, Larry, spoke for the first time since Brea had returned to the house. "My wife, she's... let's just say she's special."

"You're not the only one," Brea whispered. "You owe your daughter an explanation for why you left, why you're afraid of her. Actually, you owe all of us one."

"We aren't afraid of her," Rachelle said. "More like, we knew what would happen if we'd stayed."

"I don't understand," Brea added.

"Honey, it's complicated." Her father moved towards her, but she jerked away.

"Did you know? Did you know that they had left their thirteen-year-old daughter alone?" She turned to her father.

"No." He shook his head. "I hadn't heard from Larry and Rachelle until right before you'd called me. I didn't even know they had a daughter." He glanced around the room.

She eased up a little and sighed. So, her father hadn't condoned their actions. It still didn't make up for the fact that he'd lied to her about her mother.

She'd avoided making eye contact with the woman who'd given birth to her. It was so hard looking across the room at her mother. She'd only ever seen old pictures of her and Misty. She'd spent countless hours as a child looking at the faces of the women she wanted to know most in the world.

Her mother's face was so much different than her sister's. It might be because Misty was a ghost, or that her mother had aged so much.

Brea turned towards her mother and narrowed her eyes. "She's younger." She hadn't realized she'd spoken the words out loud until everyone turned to her.

"Who?" her mother asked.

"Misty," she answered.

Her mother's head tilted. "No, Misty was nineteen months older than me."

Brea shook her head. "No, I mean, when I saw her."

Several gasps sounded in the room. "When did you see her?" Rachelle asked.

"I've seen her several times." She turned to the woman. "Much like I saw you in my bathroom."

Rachelle stepped forward. "When? When was the first time?"

"The... the day I left Hidden Creek." She didn't tell them about teleporting back later that day.

Rachelle walked over and pulled out a large book from a bookshelf, then set it down on the kitchen table.

"What day?" she asked.

Brea thought back. "Here." She pointed to a spot on the calendar with an image of the New Moon on it.

Rachelle sighed. "It figures."

"What does?"

The woman sat down and looked around. "It's a

long story." She reached over and started dishing up a plate of spaghetti.

"One that I think you owe to us and the other people who it effects, especially your daughter," Ethan said, moving forward and putting his arm around her.

Rachelle looked around the room, then nodded. "We'll talk after dinner."

***

Ethan tried not to let his anger show as he drove back to Hidden Creek. Brea's parents were in the car behind them with Jess's parents.

"I've texted everyone to meet us at Xtina's place." Brea sat back.

"What did you tell them?" He glanced over at her.

"I opted for being vague." She glanced back nervously. "I mean, what can you say?"

"What about you? How are you holding up?" He reached over and took her hand.

He'd seen the hurt and anger on her face and had been right there with her. Even though he'd just met her father, he felt the betrayal to the core. Maybe because he was coming fresh from his own parents' secrets.

"Don't you find it ironic that all of our parents kept secrets from their kids?"

"All but Xtina's," she said, remembering what

she'd found out about them.

"Yeah, but from what my brother tells me, she didn't come out of it unscathed." He remembered talking to Mike about what Xtina's parents had done to her as a child.

"I guess when we look at the big picture, things aren't as bad as we make them out to be." He thought of what his parents had hidden from him and Mike. It was nothing compared to what Brea's dad had hidden.

By the time they pulled up at Xtina's, her driveway was almost full of cars, including his brother's police car.

Something shifted inside him, and he knew he'd been putting off really talking to the man. Something told him that tonight would be a perfect time to step aside and have that brotherly talk he needed.

"Well." Brea sighed. "Show time."

He walked around and opened her door, then took her hand and walked towards the house. They didn't even have to knock on the door before Xtina pulled it open, a frown on her face as she looked around at the people who'd followed them up to the porch. When her eyes landed on the Sorensons, her eyes narrowed and Ethan could see the anger build behind them.

"Come in," she said in a curt voice.

He followed Brea across the threshold, then

moved aside as her parents followed. When Jess's parents walked in, every eye was on her.

It was strange. He'd expected some sort of response, but Jess's face had gone completely blank. Almost like she'd known her parents who had disappeared over ten years ago would be walking into the room. Like it was a perfectly normal thing.

"Hi, sweetie," Rachelle said, rushing to her daughter, who took a step backwards.

"Jess?" Jacob moved over and took her shoulder.

"If you'll excuse me," Jess said quickly. "I have to…" She glanced around, her eyes oddly blank. Then she walked calmly from the room and disappeared into the kitchen with Xtina and Jacob on her heels.

"No." Brea stopped Jacob. "I'll go." Brea's eyes moved to her own mother. "You stay." She followed Xtina into the back. Jacob's eyes narrowed as he turned on the couple.

"The Sorensons, I presume." He took a step closer, and Ethan noticed how his brother's chest puffed out, making him look larger. Not that he needed it. Out of the three of them, only Jacob had gotten their father's impressive physic. Ethan had worked hard for years to try and achieve Jacob's muscles.

"Yes," Rachelle said, watching the hallway to the kitchen. "I should…"

Jacob stepped in front of her. "Give her time." He almost growled it out.

"I'm Mike." Mike got up, holding his hand out to Brea's father. "You're Congressmen Garrett."

"Yes, I'm Brea's father. This is my wife, Dawn."

"We had heard that you had passed." Mike glanced towards him and he nodded.

"Yes, well," Brea's father said, sighing. "I guess we all have some explaining to do. Maybe we could…" He nodded to the living room.

Mike motioned for them to sit. "Would you like something to drink?" he asked.

Jacob's bark of laughter caught everyone in the room off guard.

"Sure, offer a drink and be civil to the people who left their thirteen-year-old daughter to fend for herself," he said before storming out the front door.

Ethan held up his hand when Mike made a move to follow. "I've got this," he said, before following his brother to the front porch.

"You're pissed," he said when he found Jacob leaning against the front porch, staring out at the darkness.

"Damn right I am." He turned towards him. "I want to punch something." He crossed his arms over his chest.

"Yeah, I felt that way about an hour ago." He looked back towards the window. "Still do."

Jacob shook his head. "Do you know the kind of hell they put her through?" He ran his hands through his hair. "I was here, I remember." He closed his eyes and Ethan saw the pain in his face. "The entire town rallied behind her, so she was never really alone, but..." He shook his head and met his own eyes. "Even the pain of finding out I was adopted, abandoned by my real parents, doesn't even scratch the surface of what Jess has gone through, knowing that they had left her."

"Our family may be screwed up, but at least we've found each other now," Ethan said, leaning against the post. He turned his head towards Jacob. "That is, if you'll have us."

Jacob's eyes were still glued to the window. "Beats facing this shit alone."

Chapter Twenty-One

Brea stood by and watched Xtina comfort Jess. For her part, Jess had yet to break. Brea could see tears hiding behind her gray eyes, but so far, she was just pacing the floor.

"Are you okay?" Xtina said.

"Sure, why wouldn't I be?" She turned and stopped pacing. "My parents, who abandoned me twelve years ago, just walked in the room, acting like they had just made a run to the grocery store." She turned around and kicked the counter, then hopped up and down on her other foot. "Damn it."

"Have a seat," Xtina suggested.

"How about a glass of wine?" Xtina asked.

"A shot of whiskey is what I need," Jess said, sitting down at the table.

Xtina pulled out a bottle of wine and a bottle of Jameson and poured three glasses of each.

When she set them down, she glanced at Brea. "Are those your parents?"

"Yeah," she sighed.

"But, I thought…"

"Yeah," she interrupted, "so did I." She downed the whiskey.

Jess held up her whiskey. "May we get what we want, may we get what we need, may they get what they deserve." She downed her drink.

"Where do you get those?" Brea asked out of the blue.

"Well, that one I changed for the occasion." Jess sighed and picked up her wine glass. "It's a hobby and I have a coffee table book." She shrugged and sipped her wine.

"So, your mother isn't dead?" Xtina said after she drank down her own shot of whiskey.

"Apparently, she's been in a mental facility south of here."

"Mental?" Jess leaned forward. "Wow."

"Yeah." Brea's stomach rolled and she set her

wine glass down. "I haven't gotten the full story, but it sounds like after my aunt disappeared and I was born, she lost it." A shiver ran through her body. "Even tried to boil me alive, according to your mother." She turned to Jess. "Sounds like they used to be pretty close."

"Wow, I'm sorry." Jess turned to Xtina. "Guess all of our folks were pretty screwed up.

"Not my father," Brea added. "I mean, he lied to me my entire life, but he was a really great father."

Jess and Xtina both smiled at her. Xtina reached across and touched her hand, then pulled it away quickly. "It sounds like it." She stood up. "Well, shall we go hear their story?"

"How about another shot first?" Jess held up her shot glass.

This time, the three of them held up their glasses and all eyes moved to Jess, who smiled.

"Okay, I got one… Here's to those who treat us well, all those that don't can go to hell."

When they walked back into the living room, Xtina had a tray of drinks. Beer for the guys, and iced tea for the ladies.

Brea brought her full glass of wine as did Xtina and Jess.

She was surprised to see Ethan and Jacob walk through the front door. They looked more relaxed around each other than they had since meeting.

She took a seat and Ethan sat next to her. He grabbed a beer and downed some of it.

"You okay?" he asked quietly. She nodded in reply.

"I suppose we should start at the beginning," Rachelle said.

"Yes, why don't you." Jess stood in front of the fireplace. Jacob grabbed a beer of his own, then stood next to her.

"We were all very good friends our junior and senior years in high school," she began. Her eyes moved to Xtina. "Christina's parents too. That was until after they turned away."

"Turned away? Is that a polite way of saying they started torturing their daughter in the name of God?"

"No, before that," Dawn added. "Everything changed that night." Her eyes went to her hands.

"What night?" Xtina asked.

"The night Misty disappeared," Brea added.

"Right," Rachelle said. "The night she was chosen."

"Chosen?" Jacob stepped forward.

"Taken was more like it," Brea's father added. She could hear anger and hurt in his voice, something she'd only heard a few times before in her life.

"Taken? Chosen?" she asked. "What do you mean?"

"We had all decided to party at this place. It wasn't very well known, and not far from here."

"The silo," Xtina added.

"Yes. A bunch of football players had used a tractor to skew the lid aside. Only the popular kids knew about it. We would climb down the ladder and party."

"We'd done it several times before," Dawn added.

"What happened that night?" Mike asked.

"We were having fun; it was the last big party before winter break."

"And?" Brea said.

"I had just found my grandmother's journal. None of it made sense back then. I thought it was all some sort of joke," Rachelle said. "I thought everyone would get a kick out of it. There was a page in the back. It was all very harmless. Or so I thought." She looked down at her hands. "We did what the page said, gathered the items it required, then made a circle around the water, with the full moon overhead." She closed her eyes. "I didn't know…"

Her husband Larry reached over and took her hand in his. "How could you?" he said.

"My grandmother died when I was five. I never

got to really know her. Anyway, everyone was pretty spooked, but"—she shrugged— "we were teens. So, we said the chant, until something happened."

"What?" Xtina asked.

"The moon fell," her father added.

***

Ethan stood up quickly and glanced around the room. "You mean it's happened before?"

"No. Yes." Rachelle shook her head and looked at the others. "It's not... really."

"It's a warning," Dawn said. "Of what's to come."

"Why?" Brea asked. "What else happened that night?"

"We woke something up. Something more powerful than any of us," Rachelle said "More powerful than even my grandmother's bloodline could have ever imagined."

"I don't understand." Jess leaned forward. "What's our bloodline got to do with any of this?"

Rachelle looked at her daughter across the room. "My family, our family is very old. They were here, on this land, long before anyone else. Long before the Indians came or the pilgrims settled here."

Jess shook her head. "Before the Indians?"

Rachelle nodded her head. "From what your grandmother's journal says. Actually, it's more of a family journal." She pulled a thick book out from her bag and set it on the table in the middle of everyone. The book itself was extremely old. Its leather cover looked worn and tattered. There was a crest of sorts burned into its cover. It was about the size of a tablet, but very thick, almost a full half a foot thick. Rachelle took a deep breath. "*Apertum*," she whispered.

To everyone's amazement, except for her husband, the book's thick cover lifted and opened. The pages landed somewhere near the middle of the book.

"The spell was one of the first written. One of the first put to paper."

"Spell?" Jess's voice sounded hollow.

Rachelle's eyes met hers. "Yes,"

"Are you saying I'm almost like a witch?" Jess walked forward.

"No," Rachelle said, her eyes going to the book. "I'm saying you *are* a witch."

The room was silent, then Jess burst out laughing. "You expect me to believe what you say after you abandoned me when I was thirteen? Especially when you want me to believe that I'm a witch?" She shook her head, then moved towards the door, but Jacob's hand on her arm stopped her.

"Let's hear them out," he said, then turned to

the group. "This doesn't explain what happened to Misty."

Jess crossed her arms over her chest, but stayed in the room.

"The spell was to bring Alignak back to Earth. Alignak is the God of the moon and weather and motion. He was later worshiped by the Native Americans thanks to our family and our history with him."

"History with him?" Jacob asked.

"According to this book, he's appeared to every generation." Rachelle turned to Jess. "Now do you see why we left? You had just turned thirteen when we started noticing... things."

"What kind of things?" Jess stepped forward.

"Signs. Signs like I had gone through. We thought we could stop it. We thought that if we left..."

"That you would be protected," Jess's father added. "We continued to send Carla money each year, to pay for your apartment and everything you'd need."

"Carla knew?" Jess took a step back, looking shocked.

"She never knew where we were, or why we left, only that we had to stay away," Larry added.

Jess's eyes moved to Xtina's. She shook her head, then nodded to her parents.

Xtina paled a little, then nodded.

"Mrs. Sorenson, I'd like to try something." Xtina held out her hand for the woman's.

"Yes," Rachelle sighed. "I know what you can do. That's the main reason I allowed my daughter to be friends with you for so long."

"You hated us being friends," Jess added.

"No, we always acted like we did, but deep down, we knew it was for the best." Rachelle held out her hand. "See for yourself. Everything we've said is the truth."

Xtina reached across and touched the woman's hand. Everyone in the room watched as her green eyes sharpened for a minute or two, then Xtina dropped the woman's hand and turned her green eyes to Jess's.

"I'm sorry, Xtina said. "It's all there. The power, the sadness. It killed them to leave you."

Jess turned away from the room and Jacob walked over and wrapped his arms around her.

"So, why are you back now?" Mike asked.

"Because of what Breanna said," Rachelle said, looking towards Brea, "about seeing Misty."

"We've seen her too," Mike added. "Xtina has seen her all her life. She started appearing to me a little over a year ago."

"Then it's true. Our leaving didn't do anything." For the first time since meeting her, Ethan saw a tear form in Rachelle's eyes. "We wasted all those years." She stood up and walked to the window to look out.

"Why did you leave? I get that you were trying to protect Jess, but why leave her alone?"

"I didn't want her to grow up like I had. You don't understand. After I found my grandmother's journal, after I hit puberty, my life changed. Then I found out about my duty and my fate." She shivered visibly, then laughed. "It was instilled in me. I had one chore in my life. To pass our knowledge on to my daughter. Even that was set in stone. No sons for me, just one daughter. Period." She sniffled again as her husband wrapped his arms around her. "Just wait, you'll see. It's our curse. That and to save the world."

"And how did you save the world? By offering my aunt up as a sacrifice?" Brea asked.

Rachelle turned to Brea. "No, your aunt wasn't sacrificed." Her eyes moved to Brea's mother, Dawn. "It was an accident."

Chapter Twenty-Two

At midnight, Ethan and Brea walked across the field back to Mike's house, alone. Her parents and Jess's had gotten rooms at the hotel.

She didn't know how long they would stick around, but already, her father was talking about heading back for work the next day.

They had talked about reintroducing her mother to the public, which had made her laugh and want to tune out to their conversation.

When they entered the house, she felt the need to shut everything out, so she attacked Ethan the second the door was locked.

When she pushed him against the door, he went willingly. Her body ached to extinguish all the pain. So she used him.

When he touched her, something shifted and the hurt and pain were replaced with longing and love.

Tears slipped down her face as he carried her into the bedroom, where he made love to her slowly until she felt every ounce of hurt and pain leave her body.

"I love you," he said into her hair when she felt her own release meet his.

Her body tensed, remembering the words, remembering seeing him say them to her in another time and place. Something she'd been trying to deny was in their future.

He must have felt her tense because he shifted and looked down at her.

"I know it's so soon, but I mean it. I've never felt this way about anyone before." He brushed a strand of her hair away from her eyes.

The room was dark, with just the moonlight coming in from the window.

She could see the love in his eyes, which just broke her heart a little more.

"Ethan—"

"No, just hold on to me. I know this has been a shit day for you. I just wanted you to know that's how I felt." He leaned in and kissed her softly.

"I'm not going to change my feelings anytime soon. Let's rest." He pulled her closer and she rested her head on his shoulder. The scar was almost invisible now.

"I guess we all have a little magic in us," she said, before closing her eyes.

Once again, the dream came to her. She was standing in the field and then in the mouth of the tunnel.

This time she walked deeper into the darkness. She walked for what seemed like ten minutes until she reached a large opening. Here, the almost-red moonlight was streaming in from overhead.

She was standing in the center of the missile silo, the one everyone had been talking about. The one where her aunt had disappeared.

There wasn't any water at the base of the silo; instead, it was solid cement. Her eyes adjusted and she saw a figure standing on the other side.

Her aunt moved forward until the eerie light fell over her hair and shoulders, blocking her face from view.

"Why did you do this to me?" she asked.

Brea realized that her aunt wasn't see-through, but a solid being.

"Me? I didn't do anything." Brea took another step forward.

"You pushed me," she screamed. Then suddenly

she was across the space and directly in front of Brea, causing her to take a step back. "You're just like her." Her eyes narrowed and she could see the silver turn to white. "You're going to leave me here." Her voice rose again.

"No." Brea shook her head. "I won't. I'm trying to break you free."

Misty laughed. "There isn't a way out of the darkness." She turned away from her. Brea reached out to touch her, but her hand passed directly through the woman.

"We'll find a way. I promise. It might help to know where you are."

Her aunt turned back towards her. Then her eyes moved up until they both stood in the darkness, looking at the hunter's moon.

Brea woke when the sunlight hit her face. Turning over, she bumped into a solid wall of Ethan.

"Morning," he said, wrapping his arms around her.

"Morning." She smiled up at him.

"Did you sleep well?" he asked.

"Not really, but having you here helped." She snuggled into his warmth.

"We have about an hour before we're supposed to meet everyone in town for breakfast." He brushed his hand down her hair.

She groaned. "Do we have to?"

He pulled back and looked at her. "No, but since your folks are leaving today to head back to Atlanta, it might be for the best."

She nodded, then rolled out of bed, and he followed.

By the time they rolled into town, she had come up with a new plan.

"Will you go to the silo with me today?" she asked before he got out of the car at the diner.

"The silo? The same one my brother got shot in?"

She nodded. "I think the key to me learning how to control my ability is there."

"Why? What makes you believe that?"

"I've been dreaming about it. About a tunnel that leads to the silo."

"My brother didn't mention anything about a tunnel."

"I know. They used the main entrance and the actual missile silo. But it's there. I know it. I think I'm supposed to find it."

"Why? What would finding a tunnel have to do with all this?"

She shrugged. "It's a piece to the puzzle. One that I need to mark off my list." She waited until he walked around and opened her door. "It's a step."

He smiled and pulled her into his arms. "Of course. We'll go whenever you want. Ready?" He took her hand and they walked into the diner together.

Brea had never seen so many townspeople come out of the woodwork before. Less than fifteen minutes after Jess's parents walked in, the entire town of Hidden Creek was crowded into the diner.

Some had choice words for the couple, but for the most part, people were just happy they were back, safe and sound.

Jess sat in the corner of the booth across from Ethan and Brea, with Jacob by her side, almost guarding her. When people came over to chat with her about her parents' return, Jacob would dismiss them quickly.

"He's kind of like a big guard dog," Ethan whispered into her ear. She chuckled and Jess and Jacob looked across the small space at her.

"How are you holding up?" she asked Jess.

"Okay, I guess. I'm sorry about what they put you through. At least I knew my parents were alive." She shook her head. "It must be a lot harder having someone you believed dead all your life turn out to be alive." She glanced over at Brea's parents sitting at a table not far from the booth.

"It was quite a shock." She glanced over at Jess.

"Actually, I'd like to kick something."

Jess chuckled. "It doesn't help, just hurts." She reached down and rubbed her leg.

The door of the diner opened and Brea glanced around to see a tall blond man walk in. He took in everyone in the room, then headed towards their booth.

"Hey, Joe," Jacob said.

"Did you read this?" Joe held up a newspaper in front of him. He looked at Brea and his eyes narrowed. "You're Breanna Garrett. Good job destroying this town." Joe tossed the paper down, then turned and left.

"What's he talking about?" Jess asked, reaching for the paper. But Brea had already seen the headline and groaned. Mentally she traced back to the last time she'd opened the article. Just before her meeting with Drew at the library. She'd put it on her USB drive. Reaching down to her purse, she found the side pocket empty and groaned. She should have guessed. Drew had known about her hiding spot. After all, they had dated for several months.

After this, there was no way she was going to work with him ever again.

She glanced over as Jess picked up the paper.

"Small town of Hidden Creek full of crackpots and kooks. By Breanna Garrett."

***

"Did you write this?" Jess asked Brea after scanning the story.

"Yes and no. I wrote it, the first week I was in town, but I never submitted it," Brea said. "Drew took my USB drive. The story was on it."

"That…" Ethan thought of a million names to call him.

Brea put her hand on his arm and stopped him.

"What does it say?" Ethan asked.

"That's not my title, but it pretty much sums the story up." She sighed. "It sucks that the first piece I've gotten published is that one."

He took the paper from Jess and scanned it. A large picture of her was beside the title, no doubt to make sure everyone in town knew who she was. He felt Brea cringe when he got to the part about his brothers, and he chuckled slightly. "Great writing," he said, setting the paper down. "Congratulations on getting published."

"That's it?" She turned to him. "After reading that, that's all you have to say?"

"What do you want me to say? That was before everything… happened." He shrugged. "You can't be blamed for having an opinion." He took her hand, meaning every word.

"I don't really see how this could be a bad thing for Hidden Creek," Jess said, causing everyone at the table to look at her. "I mean, sure, it says that

253

we're all delusional but, other than that, what's Joe all worked up about?"

Brea sighed. "He's probably upset about the part about the Neanderthal liquor store worker."

Jess laughed. "I liked that part. Forget about it. Hey, at least now you might start getting job offers."

Brea smiled. "Yeah, I never thought about it that way. At least my ex had the decency to keep my name on it and not take credit."

Ethan reached over and took her hand, then pulled it up to his lips. "You're pretty amazing."

He stood by and watched her say goodbye to her parents. He'd experienced awkward before, but nothing like her saying goodbye to her dad. He could tell she was still hurting but had sucked it up to send them off.

Jess's parents were staying in town for a while longer. Her father had a job at the local brewery just outside of The Rock and had limited time off. The way Jess was acting around them, he could tell that she would have preferred them gone already. Who could really blame her?

He still wasn't sure how he was going to act when he saw his folks again. The betrayal in this town was something legends were made of.

Jacob climbed back in his patrol car and Jess walked back to the Coffee Corner, leaving them with Xtina and Mike.

"So?" Mike set the paper down. "Good job." He smiled over at Brea. "You've a talent for telling a story."

Brea sighed. "So, none of you are mad?"

"Why would we be? It's a beautiful piece. Besides, it's the truth from an outsider's perspective," Xtina answered. "I think you may have just found your new calling."

"I've never known anyone like you guys before." Brea shook her head.

He reached around and wrapped his arm around her shoulders to pull her closer. "We'll take that as a compliment, right?" Everyone in the booth nodded.

"We were going to go and look around the silo a little more today. You know, see if there's something we can find out," he said to everyone.

"We've been there a few more times. I still can't seem to make it past one room," Xtina said, cringing.

"Why?" Brea shifted forward slightly.

"Something... blinds me." Xtina frowned.

"Blinds?" Ethan asked.

"When I get close to the room, a searing white light causes me pain." She tapped the side of her head. "We were going to try going in from the missile spot instead of the main door to see if we could bypass it. I'd really like to see the rest of the place, even though..." He saw her shiver, then his brother reached over and held her.

"It's okay, we don't have to," Mike said.

"We've been over this. The answer is there. We just need to look harder," Xtina said.

"Why do you think the answer is there?"

"I can feel it," Xtina said. "And something is drawing me there."

Brea visibly shivered. "The cave," she whispered.

"Cave? What cave?" Xtina asked.

She shook her head. "It's actually a tunnel. I've seen it."

Mike leaned forward. "We haven't found a tunnel."

"There is one. I've been there."

"Then we'll go with you," Mike said. "We have a few things to do first. How about we meet you at the house at noon?"

"Sounds good," Ethan said. "Shall we head out?" He helped Brea out of the booth.

When they paid, Carla smiled and held up a newspaper. "Well, it looks like we have a celebrity in our midst. It was a really great article." She leaned forward and patted Brea on the arm. "We all think so. You've put Hidden Creek on the map."

Brea looked a little shocked, but then smiled and said thank you.

They held hands as they walked out to her car.

"I still can't believe no one is mad." She shook her head.

He chuckled. "Small towns tend to stick up for their own."

He wasn't surprised to see Drew leaning on her car. The man's arms were crossed over his chest like he was proud of what he'd done. Ethan wanted to smash the guy's face in, but held back.

Brea smiled brightly when she noticed him.

"Well, Drew. It seems I owe you a thanks."

The man's smile faltered a little. "For?"

"The article." She dropped his hand and walked over to Drew. He stood back to watch the show. "Everyone in town is saying how much they loved it. Whatever your intentions, thank you." She moved around him and climbed into the passenger side.

Ethan stepped closer. "Why are you still in town?" His eyes narrowed. "There's nothing for you here." The man's eyes went to Brea. "Not anymore." He moved around him and got in the driver side. When he pulled the car out of the parking lot, Drew watched them closely.

"Do you really think he did you a favor?" he asked when they were outside of town.

"Yeah, I mean, I'd never thought about writing before. Ever since I could remember, I wanted to be a journalist, but for some reason, always thought I'd be in front of a camera. Now it's like more doors are opened." She was quiet for a moment, then turned to him. "What about you?"

"Me?" He glanced at her.

"Sure, I mean, Mike said you're on leave for your injury, but now… with everything the way it is, what are you going to do?"

What was he going to do? He hadn't thought of it. He'd told Brea that he loved her, something he had never said to anyone before. Surley what was cause to reevaluate his life.

Mike and Xtina had announced to everyone that they were now officially engaged but hadn't set the date. He'd never thought of marriage, having a family, or settling down. His entire existence was to fight, be a warrior. He didn't think he could be a husband, a father, or even have a normal job.

"I'm not sure," he said. "I guess I've never really thought about it."

"What about the police force? Jacob was talking about needing more men now that two of the guys are up for retirement," she said, glancing out the window as they drove up to the house. "I may not know where I'll be working, but it's clear to me that I don't belong in the city anymore."

"You're moving here?" he asked, putting the car into park.

"Why not? With everything crazy going on, I'm not even sure there will be a tomorrow, but I know one thing, I can't imagine going back to my boring life after all this."

Chapter Twenty-Three

They spent the next two hours hunched over her computer searching for old plans of silos built in Georgia. There were several different basic government plans, but none of them called for a tunnel. Most of them had the missiles loading directly into the silo itself.

They did find a plan that called for an access tunnel for heavy equipment, but from what Mike and Xtina had told them about the place, it didn't seem like it would fit this one.

Still, they printed several plans and changed into appropriate clothing to go exploring. They headed over to Xtina's house just before noon.

When they got there, she had a plate of sandwiches and iced tea waiting for them.

"I figured we'd better fuel up before heading over there. It's pretty big and you tend to lose track of time. We've packed water too."

They all sat in the kitchen and ate, while Ethan and Mike went over the plans they had printed out.

"The closest plan is this one," Mike said. He glanced up at her. "But there's no tunnel."

"If there is one, we'll find it," Xtina said, smiling at her.

When they headed out, Mike and Ethan both had backpacks on their backs filled with water, flashlights, and emergency supplies.

It took almost an hour to walk to the main opening. The door had several thick locks on it, but Mike pulled out a key ring and started opening them.

"Jacob." He smiled. "It pays to have a brother in law enforcement."

"What about going in through the silo?" Brea asked.

"We talked it over and thought that for your first visit, it would be best for you to enter the easy way. Some of the rungs on the ladder are a little sketchy." His eyes met Ethan's.

She crossed her arms over her chest. "You don't think us women can handle climbing down a ladder?"

Xtina turned to Mike. "Is that true?"

"Oh, it's true. Just look into those eyes. They're hiding something," Brea added.

Xtina crossed her arms over her chest and narrowed her eyes at Mike.

Mike sighed and looked at Ethan, who, to his credit, just shrugged.

"Okay, if it's what you want."

"I want Xtina to be able to explore the place, and if that means going in through the silo, then I'm game," Brea said.

Xtina smiled over at her. "Thanks." She turned to Mike. "Well?"

He chuckled. "Fine, let's go." He finished unlocking the door. "In case we decide to leave this way," he said, then he took Xtina's hand in his. They started walking again.

It took them almost ten minutes to reach the large circular cover. The two massive metal hydraulic doors were opened slightly.

"This is the tricky part," Mike said. "I'll go first, then help the ladies down." He tossed his bag to the bottom of the shaft. Ethan's bag followed.

They all stood by and watched Mike wedge his body around the opening and then dangle by just his arms as he kicked his feet out and caught the ladder. It took him less than a minute to disappear into the hole.

"Okay, Xtina you're next. Just do what I did. I'm right here and will guide you to the ladder."

Xtina took a deep breath and followed his lead.

Suddenly, Brea had doubts about all this and took a step back.

"Hey." Ethan was right beside her. "If you don't want…"

She shook her head. "No. I… I can do this."

His hands covered hers. "You've got this."

She nodded.

"Okay, ready for you, Brea," Mike called up.

She wiped her sweaty hands on her jeans and took a deep breath.

"Okay, I'm coming down." She lay down on her belly on the cold metal, her legs dangling in the opening. She shimmied until her hips were at the edge of the opening, then continued until she was hanging over the edge.

Ethan was holding her hands and she knew he would never let her go, not until he knew she was safe.

Kicking her feet towards the edge, she felt Mike's hands wrap around her ankles.

"Gotcha," he said. She was passed from one brother to the other so quickly, a small scream escaped her lips. She laughed when she wrapped her arms around Mike and chuckled into his chest.

"What a ride," she said as her feet touched the first rung.

"Yeah, you should try doing it in the dark and

when it's raining," he joked.

"Head on down." He nodded to the tall ladder. "Go slow, take your time. Test each rung before putting your full weight on it."

She nodded, then moved around him, their bodies sliding across one another's. She instantly compared his body to Ethan's. They were the same, but… different.

Her body responded to his touch, but nothing like it did when Ethan touched her. As she climbed down slowly, she ran over what her mind was telling her.

Thoughts of another man touching her like Ethan did were blocked from her mind. She couldn't imagine it. Not after what he'd said to her.

He loved her. Did she love him? That question had been running over and over in her mind since last night. She'd never loved anyone other than her father.

When her feet hit the ground, she glanced up in time to see Ethan's feet hanging over the opening. Her breath held until his feet gripped the ladder. She hadn't realized how tall the silo was and instantly felt fear for him and Mike as they took their time climbing down the ladder.

"Wow," Xtina said, glancing around. "It's massive."

Her eyes moved around the silo while her mind focused on worry for the men.

Xtina was right. The place was huge. There was a foul smell of stale water and rusted metal.

"We found Rose here." Xtina looked to the middle of the floor. "She'd fallen down the opening."

"Wow, I can't imagine falling that far." Her eyes moved back up to the opening.

"I know, we were lucky she survived." Xtina turned to her. "Actually, it was your aunt that led us to her."

"Misty?"

Xtina smiled as Mike reached the bottom. "Yes, she woke us and led us here."

"Why?"

"We're not sure," Mike said, picking up his pack. "But we're thankful. We love Rose."

Ethan hit the bottom and walked over to her. "You okay?"

She nodded. "Yes, but I think we'll leave the other way." She smiled.

They followed Mike around the main silo area.

"There are a couple rooms off of the silo, but they are all small storage areas and don't lead anywhere. The main hallway is there." He pointed his flashlight to a large opening.

A shiver ran through Brea, and she felt something beckoning her down the circular hallway.

"There," she said, her eyes glued to the spot.

Everyone was silent for a moment.

"What do you feel?" Xtina asked.

"Something." She shook her head. "It's this way." She moved towards the opening, and Ethan laid his hand on her arm. "I'm okay." Her eyes met his. He nodded and dropped his hand.

"We'll follow you," Xtina said.

Brea let it pull her down the dark corridors, through several bunker-style rooms. There was old furniture in some rooms, and graffiti covered almost every wall.

They must have walked for half an hour, climbing stairs, entering hallway after hallway.

"I never found this side of it," Mike said when she'd opened an old metal door. It had taken both Mike and Ethan to pry the rusted door open.

Here, the walls were not as covered with graffiti.

"I don't think many knew about this part," Ethan said, his flashlight going over each wall. "The graffiti stopped about twenty years ago."

Brea moved again. She could hear her heart beat in her head and felt her mind drawing her to one goal.

She stopped in front of a door and her entire

266

body shivered.

"It's here," she whispered.

"What?" Xtina asked.

"I don't know, but whatever it is, it's powerful."

Ethan walked around her and tried the door. "Mike." He nodded. The men worked on the door.

"There's no graffiti," Xtina said.

Brea turned and glanced around the walls herself. They were blank, cement walls. The room they were standing in appeared not to have been disturbed since the military packed up and left it.

She turned when she heard the door squeak open. A light shone into the tunnel from the room.

Brea stepped slowly into the tunnel from her dreams, knowing now that fate was inevitable.

***

Ethan watched Brea closely. The tunnel was long, and just the faintest of lights could be seen from around the corner, signaling that the sunlight was getting in through an opening somewhere.

Instead of walking towards the opening, Brea stopped a few feet in and turned around.

"Somethings different." She frowned.

"What?" Xtina asked.

"I... I don't know." She turned around.

"Maybe I can help?" Xtina said.

"How?" Brea turned to her.

As an answer, Xtina held out her hands. Brea nodded, then placed her hands in Xtina's.

Ethan and Mike stood by and watched them. Both of their eyes grew distant. When they dropped their hands, Xtina sighed.

"You entered from there." She nodded to the opening. "Not from here. Let's try that."

They walked to the end of the tunnel. The tree branches and grass had grown up over the opening. It took them several minutes to clear a pathway.

Finally, they stood on the outside of the metal gate opening, looking around.

"I can't believe we didn't find this the first time," Mike said to Xtina.

"We're more than a mile away from the silo," she said in reply.

"The place is bigger than we thought." Mike turned to Brea. "Well?"

Brea had gone pale.

Without saying anything, she started to move forward, as if in a trance. They followed her without a word.

They thought she would stop in the tunnel again, but instead, she returned to the room they had just left, then proceeded to follow the path they had just taken all the way back to the silo. By the time they entered the massive room, the sky had grown dark. Still no one had spoken a word.

Brea stood in the center of the silo, then raised her hands above her head. "*Apertus,*" she said, and to everyone's shock, the giant metal doors slowly lifted until they were fully open. Brea turned to Xtina, her silver eyes almost glowing in the fading light. "*Primum,*" she said, then Ethan watched in horror as her eyes rolled to the back of her head. He reached her just before she landed on the cold cement floor of the empty silo.

They carried her out the main entrance. Her body had turned cold. When they reached the spot where Xtina cried out in pain, Mike hoisted her over his shoulders and carried her out of the bunker the rest of the way.

"What the hell?" he said when he laid Brea gently down in the front car seat.

"I'm better," Xtina said when they were finally outside.

"What was that?" Mike asked, running his hands through his hair.

"I don't know," Xtina said, taking a drink of the water Mike offered her.

Ethan's eyes were still on Brea. Her coloring was a little better, but still, she was so cold. "Brea?" He slapped her cheek lightly. "Brea?"

Her eyes fluttered and then opened. "Ethan?"

He sighed and gathered her close. "Are you

okay?"

"What happened?" she asked.

"You told the silo doors to open in Latin, and they did." Xtina shook her head. "Then you said… 'Soon,' I think. I'll want to check my translation just to make sure."

"You know Latin?" Mike asked her.

"Sure." She shrugged. "It helps when you're ten and banishing the dead from your room."

Mike leaned in and kissed Xtina on the lips. "That's such a turn on." He gathered her close.

Ethan turned back to Brea, brushing a strand of hair from her eyes. "How about you?"

She shook her head. "Never learned Latin. The last thing I remember is standing outside of the tunnel."

"Maybe we should give it a rest?" Mike suggested.

"No." Brea stood up. He tried to help her, but she pushed him away. "Time is running out." She looked up to the dark sky. "If we don't figure this out soon…" Her unspoken words hung in the air. Everyone standing there knew what was coming.

"We can't solve anything tonight. Both of you were just…" Mike kicked a clump of dirt in frustration. "Damn it. We can't keep doing this."

"Mike." Xtina rushed over to him and laid a hand on his arm. "We'll figure this out."

"I need to go back," Brea said, walking towards the opening.

"Like hell." Ethan followed her into the field and then pulled her to a stop. Something close to déjà vu passed quickly in his mind. "Stop." He pulled her into his arms. "I can't see you like that again." He held onto her.

"Ethan, I have to. The answer's there." She sighed into his chest.

He pulled back and looked down at her. "I love you. I can't see you like this. It's killing me."

She smiled at him. "I love you, too."

He felt like his heart had finally started beating as warmth spread through him. "You do?"

She smiled. "Of course. I've loved you from the moment I first dreamed of you. I feel like we've known each other forever. I want nothing more than to spend the rest of our lives together, but before any of that can happen, there's something I have to do."

He shook his head. "We can go away from here. Leave all this craziness behind. Spend the rest of our lives together."

She shook her head. "No, we can't." She took a step away from him, her smile fading. "You have to let me go." She took another step back.

He dropped his arms when the memory hit him. "No." He shook his head. "Not like this."

She stepped further away from him, her eyes running over his face. She reached up towards him, but she was too far away to touch him. "I love you, but I have to go."

"Why?" he asked, but he knew he wouldn't get an answer.

She took another step back, then looked up at the sky. His gaze followed and when he found the sliver of the moon, he looked at her again. She was less than two feet away from him, but he knew he wouldn't be able to get to her in time.

Her eyes turned back to him as her hand reached out for him, then she screamed, no.

He stood there in the dark field, with the waxing moon overhead, and watched her fade from his life.

The Beckoning

273

The Ascension

Jess has been fighting the fate she's known all her life. She hasn't allowed seeing her own death put a damper on her life. But now that her time is starting to come closer, she has to make the decision to fight it, or save the world.

Other books by Jill Sanders

The Pride Series
Finding Pride
Discovering Pride
Returning Pride
Lasting Pride
Serving Pride
Red Hot Christmas
My Sweet Valentine
Return To Me
Rescue Me

The Secret Series
Secret Seduction
Secret Pleasure
Secret Guardian
Secret Passions
Secret Identity
Secret Sauce

The West Series
Loving Lauren
Taming Alex
Holding Haley
Missy's Moment
Breaking Travis
Roping Ryan
Wild Bride
Corey's Catch

The Grayton Series

Last Resort
Someday Beach
Rip Current
In Too Deep
Swept Away

Lucky Series
Unlucky In Love
Sweet Resolve

Silver Cove Series
Silver Lining
French Kiss

Entangled Series – *Paranormal Romance*
The Awakening
The Beckoning
The Ascension… Coming Soon

For a complete list of books: http://jillsanders.com

This is a work of fiction. Names, characters, places, and incidents are either the product of the author's imagination or are used fictitiously, and any resemblance to actual persons, living or dead, business establishments, events, or locales is entirely coincidental.

THE BECKONING
PRINT ISBN: 978-1-942896-77-7
DIGITAL ISBN: 978-1-942896-76-0
Copyright © 2016 Jill Sanders

About the Author

Jill Sanders is *The New York Times* and *USA Today* bestselling author of the Pride Series, Secret Series, West Series, Grayton Series, Lucky Series, and Silver Cove romance novels. She continues to lure new readers with her sweet and sexy stories. Her books are available in every English-speaking country and in audiobooks as well as being translated into different languages.

Born as an identical twin to a large family, she was raised in the Pacific Northwest and later relocated to Colorado for college and a successful IT career before discovering her talent as a writer. She now makes her home along the Emerald Coast in Florida where she enjoys the beach, hiking, swimming, wine tasting, and of course writing.

Connect with Jill on Facebook:
http://fb.com/JillSandersBooks

Twitter: @JillMSanders or visit her Web site at
http://JillSanders.com